NO LONGER PROPERTY OF
ANYTHINK LIBRARIES/
RANGEVIEW LIBRARY DISTRICT

# SCULPTING
*Anna*

## BY

## VENUS REISING

Bella
BOOK

201

Copyright © 2015 by Venus Reising

Bella Books, Inc.
P.O. Box 10543
Tallahassee, FL 32302

All rights reserved. No part of this book may be reproduced or transmitted in any form or by any means, electronic or mechanical, including photocopying, without permission in writing from the publisher.

This is a work of fiction. Names, characters, businesses, places, events and incidents are either the products of the author's imagination or used in a fictitious manner. Any resemblance to actual persons, living or dead, or actual events is purely coincidental. The publisher does not have any control over and does not assume any responsibility for author or third-party websites or their content.

Printed in the United States of America on acid-free paper.

First Bella Books Edition 2015

Editor: Medora MacDougall
Cover Designer: Judith Fellows

ISBN: 978-1-59493-447-6

*PUBLISHER'S NOTE*
*The scanning, uploading, and distribution of this book via the Internet or via any other means without the permission of the publisher is illegal and punishable by law. Please purchase only authorized electronic editions, and do not participate in or encourage electronic piracy of copyrighted materials. Your support of the author's rights is appreciated.*

## About the Author

Venus Reising is the alter ego of a writing duo out of Orlando, Florida. The literary twosome is one-half professor, with poetry and criticism published in numerous journals, including *Ascent Aspirations*, *Falling Star* and *Atlantic Literary Review*, and one-half working artist turned pre-med student, who has, at least for now, traded her canvas for a periodic table. Partners in writing and in life, the Venus women would much rather interrogate characters and complicate plots than do just about anything else.

## Dedications

To my mother, who didn't sell me to the gypsies when I "practiced my writing" on her antique furniture, and to Dr. E, who "corrected" the pronouns in my first attempt at a love story: it was *she*.

–S

To my mother, who read every one of the silly mysteries I wrote as a child, and to both my parents, who taught me to dream big, love fully and never give up. Thank you for always believing in me.

–D

## Acknowledgments

The library in Neil Gaiman's *Sandman* holds all the novels never written or never finished, except in dreams. This book would be on the shelves of that library if it were not for the support of some fabulous people. Thanks, first, to the magical Medora MacDougall for using her fairy dust to make our toad of a story more *princessy*. You're a phenomenal editor, writer and teacher, Medora, and you have Minnesota kindness to boot. Thanks to Karin Kallmaker and Bella Books for taking a chance on two inexperienced storytellers with a crazy plotline and far too much enthusiasm for their own good. Thanks to our writing friends for encouraging us to keep typing through many hand cramps and bouts of self-doubt. Thanks to our families for their continuous love and support. And thank you, dear readers, for spending time with us in our crazy zoo. We're so glad to have you along for the ride! And please *do* feed the animals.

# CHAPTER ONE

Lexy Strayer held the Styrofoam cup under the sputtering nozzle of the instant coffee vending machine while attempting to hold in place thirty fresh-off-the-copier syllabi for her morning composition class between her left elbow and her hip and a recently watered bamboo plant in her left hand. Her key chain was hooked onto her index finger and half a toasted bagel slathered with cream cheese was clamped in her jaw. She could feel some of the papers slipping from the stack, and as she shifted to try to prevent impending disaster, she heard a female voice from behind her.

"Need some help?"

A woman clad in jeans and a hippie-style tunic grabbed hold of the syllabi before they fell to the floor. Lexy attempted to speak with the bagel still lodged between her teeth. Her "thank you" came out more like a "Harrumph."

"Here you go." The dark-haired woman held the stack triumphantly out to Lexy, who had since set the coffee, which decidedly looked more like diesel fuel than cappuccino, down on the window ledge and removed her breakfast from her mouth.

Lexy smiled. "Thank you. I guess I'm guilty of over-tasking."

The woman's green eyes sparkled under the normally unflattering fluorescent bulbs overhead. "You're Professor Strayer, right?"

"Guilty as charged." Lexy wiped the corner of her mouth with her index finger, fearing that she may have unwittingly painted her lips with cream cheese during the fiasco.

"I'm Anna Stevens." The young woman's smile was a bit lopsided, Lexy noticed, slightly higher on the left side, cresting at an adorable dimple. Her complexion was lighter than Lexy's own olive one and the skin around her eyes and mouth was absent the light wrinkles reflected by Lexy's mirror each morning. "I'm in your Introduction to Literature class this afternoon."

Lexy chastised herself for allowing her eyes to roam to the young woman's soft full lips, lingering there for a moment before snapping back to the deep green irises. She felt her face flush. Time for a fast retreat, she thought. "Nice to meet you, Anna," she said, tucking an errant strand of honey-brown hair back into the loose French braid she wore. "I guess I'll see you then." Taking her stack of papers from the woman's arms, she shuffled off to her office to deposit the bamboo before heading to Franklin Hall.

* * *

Anna watched Professor Strayer's retreat down the hallway. She couldn't help but check her out—long legs in tan tailored pants and a fitted white blouse that showed off her sexy physique. "My prof is a hottie," she whispered to herself as she unfolded her schedule to find the location of her first class. Slinging her backpack over her right shoulder, she headed toward the quad.

* * *

"So, did you meet the newbie yet?" Jennifer sipped her foamy café mocha and looked quizzically at Lexy.

This was Jennifer's last year on tenure track at Orange County College in Orlando, the largest two-year college in the Southeast. Lexy anticipated that, armed with a continuing contract the next fall, Jennifer would stop agreeing to every project their dean threw her way, begin nailing some paintings to the walls of her office, and trade her usual blazers, pantyhose and heels for jeans and flip-flops. Of course, knowing her friend, Lexy expected that the jeans would be top of the line designer ones and the flip-flops would be by Prada.

During Jennifer's first few years at OCC, she and Lexy had shared an office and had become close, especially after realizing that they were the only lesbians in the English Department. Unfortunately, the subject was broached when Jennifer made a shameless and fruitless pass at Lexy while they were preparing the set for a student theater production of *Our Town*.

"What newbie?" Lexy asked as she jealously watched her friend sip her high-calorie drink. Jennifer's curvaceous figure could never appear fat, and no matter what the woman ate, her weight never seemed to fluctuate. Lexy sipped her own black coffee, frowning.

"The new four-monther. Cole."

Temporary full-time positions were referred to as four-month contracts since faculty who held such positions were not guaranteed employment after the semester was over. If she had been in town, Lexy would have met the new faculty member at the Academic Assembly held each August prior to the start of classes, but she had extended her visit with her mother in Maine instead.

Her mother's second husband, Carl, had passed away six months earlier, and she hadn't been adjusting well. She and Carl owned a hobby shop, to which he contributed his own hand-made dollhouse furniture. When Lexy had visited in August, her mother had shown her some of his handiwork, a miniature kitchen table and chairs that looked just like the one they were sitting at as they drank their tea that morning. Looking at the tiny replica in her mother's palm made Lexy feel unsettled, as though she had fallen through some sort of metaphorical rabbit hole or something.

"I don't know how I'll get on without him," her mother had said, studying the delicate chenille-striped seat cushions.

"I know." Lexy had patted her hand and was surprised by how soft and thin her skin felt and the way her flesh moved across the bones and tendons like liquid waves. "You will get through it, Mom, just like I did."

Lexy had lost her partner, Jules, to breast cancer four years earlier. She wasn't honestly sure that she had, in fact, gotten through it, nor was she sure what that phrase even meant.

Jennifer turned searching eyes on Lexy. "Well?" she asked, growing impatient with her friend's disinterest in the conversation.

"No, I haven't met the newbie yet. What's he like?"

"She," Jennifer corrected. "*Andrea* Cole." The way Jennifer's eyebrows raised as she pronounced the woman's name made it obvious that she found the new four-monther attractive. "I think she's one of us," Jennifer whispered while seductively licking off her upper lip the milky froth from her last sip of coffee.

"You're shameless, you know that? Besides, what are the chances that of seven full-time English instructors, three are gay?"

"Slim. But I'm telling you, she gave me the once-over."

"You're imagining things."

"Scout's honor." Jennifer lifted two fingers up to her forehead in some sort of melodramatic salute.

"Give it up. You were never even a Brownie."

"So? It's a common expression. Anyway, that's beside the point. When Keith introduced us, I'm telling you the woman held my hand too long for a normal shake and her eyes raked over me. I thought I was going to melt into a puddle at the feet of her tall, dark and handsome self."

Lexy had watched Jennifer jump into bed with anything that had breasts and a pulse since Samantha left her two years ago for her *male* yoga instructor. Jennifer claimed that meaningless sex was therapeutic, but Lexy thought otherwise, which is one of the reasons why she had promptly cooled her friend's advances when they were directed at her just after the breakup.

"You know, it's probably not a good idea to get involved with a colleague. Remember the Jacquie fiasco?" Jennifer had slept with the straight but curious adjunct in the art department after the college's winter holiday party last year. Which led to Marc, Jacquie's angry fiancé, demonstrating just how efficiently a properly swung golf club can demolish the windows of a BMW.

"A girl can dream, can't she?" Jennifer gave Lexy a long look. "So...how's the dating scene, Lexy Loner?"

"Nonexistent as usual." Lexy paused, remembering that morning's vending machine meeting with Anna, and added with a groan, "Actually, I caught myself checking out a student today. How pathetic am I?"

"Oh my! How old?"

"Does it matter? She's a *student!*"

"Hot?"

Lexy laughed, throwing a balled-up napkin at her friend. "Stop it!"

"Well, let's plan to go out Friday night then. We'll see if we can't find you a legal prospect."

"I don't know," Lexy said noncommittally. Just thinking about the meat-market feel of the local lesbian bars filled her with revulsion.

"It's time you got back in the game, Lex. Jules has been gone for four years."

The mere mention of her name caused a painful lump to form in Lexy's throat. It wasn't just Jennifer who had started to needle her about diving back into the dating pool. Even her own mother, the same woman who, after learning that she was a lesbian, served her an annotated Bible and pamphlets on conversion therapy for breakfast, had begun encouraging her to go out to meet women. Apparently, Lexy'd exceeded the permissible mourning time and had tipped the scales into *Grey Gardens* territory. But four years wasn't enough. No number of years would ever be enough.

Jennifer began collecting her belongings. "I'm off to frighten another class of freshmen who think they're writing the next *Harry Potter* or *Hunger Games* series. I'll call you later."

\* \* \*

Anna answered her cell on the second ring. "Hello?"

"Hey, sweetie." She could hear Ian smiling through the phone.

She and Ian had been best friends since they'd become next-door neighbors in Tallahassee when she was five. They'd bonded over G.I. Joe and couch cushion forts, and they even had their own secret handshake. In high school, they found something else they had in common: They were both gay.

"Hi, E."

"I know you're busy with school and all, but Cayden insisted on calling his mommy to tell her that he won a potato sack race at preschool today."

When Ian and his partner Christian were considering having a child together, it seemed only natural that he would ask her. And it was equally natural that she would say yes.

"Well, I would expect no less with his amazing genes."

Ian laughed. "Hold on. I'll put him on."

"We won! We won!" Cayden shouted into the mouthpiece.

"That's so wonderful!" Anna said, yanking the phone away from her ear to protect her hearing. "You're amazing, Cayden!"

"And I got a ribbon!"

"Wow!" It sounded as though Cayden was jumping up and down; the thought made Anna smile uncontrollably. Then, per his usual, he dropped the phone. A muffled sound followed.

"Sorry about that," Ian said. "Anyway, I know you've got classes so I'll let you go, but we love you, sweet cheeks. Best of luck on your new venture."

"I love you guys too, E. Thanks for thinking of me."

\* \* \*

Anna chose a seat in the back of the classroom. She was tempted to check her phone's voice mail but thought better of it when she saw Professor Strayer look up sharply from her briefcase when a cell phone elsewhere in the room emitted a muffled Kelly Clarkson ringtone.

"Be forewarned," the professor said. "If that happens again, I *will* answer it."

Anna's morning class, US Government, hadn't been too bad. The professor, who introduced himself as John, was younger and more hip than she had expected him to be. It didn't take Anna long to realize why he had a lot of chili peppers on the Professor Rater website. The class was full of women ogling his jeans-clad ass as he wrote his name and office hours on the board. In fact, she seemed to be the only female in the room *not* doing so. That would not be the case, she thought, if Professor Strayer had a lot of notes to write on the board. That she wouldn't mind at all.

Anna was nervous about returning to school after a hiatus of ten years. Her mother, a single parent, had suffered a debilitating stroke shortly after Anna's eighteenth birthday. She surrendered her scholarship to Vassar in order to take care of her. Despite the months of physical therapy, her mother never regained the lost mobility and function. The difficulty of maneuvering in and out of locations ill-equipped for wheelchairs and the potential clients who shied away from her garbled speech effectively ended her career as a realtor. Anna, who was already working in a frame shop, picked up a second job as a bartender to cover the household bills and help pay the portion of the mortgage that disability didn't. She had struggled to take classes at Tallahassee Community College for two semesters but dropped out thereafter.

At twenty-eight, Anna was older than the majority of her classmates, but so far she didn't feel too out of place. She had even made a couple acquaintances that could potentially become friendships. Glancing around this classroom now, however, she found no familiar faces, aside from that of the instructor, of course, who seemed less frazzled and more at ease at the front of the classroom than she had earlier at the vending machines.

Professor Strayer smoothed a few fallen hairs back and picked up a stack of papers at the front of the room. She walked carefully through the room, as if worried about potential collisions with the corners of the trapezoid-shaped tables, and handed each student a stapled packet. When she arrived at Anna's seat, she smiled and gave a slight nod of acknowledgment.

Inwardly, Anna was beaming. She liked the fact that she had been singled out—that she had shared a moment with Professor Strayer that no one else was privy to.

\* \* \*

Lexy hated the first day of classes. The students were always uncharacteristically quiet, all of them facing front with their notebooks open and their highlighter pens at the ready like little soldiers. Even after a decade of teaching, she still felt the chaotic butterflies in the pit of her stomach on the first day.

She introduced herself, cataloguing her degrees, teaching experience and contact information, and then segued into the obligatory recitation of classroom policies. After eight years at OCC, this part of her opening day spiel had become second nature to her, and she found her attention drifting as she discussed attendance.

"Class meets Mondays and Wednesdays. Please try to arrive promptly at one. I allow three absences, but after the third one, ten percent will be deducted from your attendance grade. You have three freebies. Use them wisely…"

She continued by rote, her eyes scanning the room until stopped by attentive deep green ones, and then drifting downward to linger again on those soft, full lips. Lips which were currently chewing on the end of a mechanical pencil.

Lexy felt heat prickle her skin. *What the hell is wrong with me? I'm probably old enough to be her mother. For Christ's sake, get a grip!* She had always conducted herself professionally while at school, especially in the classroom. Some of her colleagues were known to invite their students to their homes for dinner parties or "hang out" with them in the college cafeteria. But not Lexy. She worked hard to maintain her professional distance. She had certainly never felt an attraction toward a student before.

And she didn't now, she told herself. It must be some weird hormonal blip in her system. Come to think of it, she *had* been renting a lot of romantic comedies and craving chocolate lately. She shook her head. Time to get to work.

Lexy started all of her classes with the same icebreaker activity, which she conducted in the process of taking roll. She had her students write down three statements about themselves, two of them true and one a lie. Every student would read his or her statements and the rest of the class would try to determine which one was false. This Introduction to Literature class was relatively small, so she expected to be able to dismiss the students early. That was good since she hadn't had a chance to eat lunch yet and her stomach was rumbling.

"Jenna Adams?" she asked, reading from the roster.

A young bottle-blonde in the front row giggled as she read her statements. "I have two brothers. I'm sixteen. I just moved to Florida two months ago."

Lexy liked this activity because she could easily determine who the class clowns would be.

"Sixteen?" piped up a boy with a mohawk that was streaked fire truck red. "Watch out for her, guys. Statutory rape!"

*And there's the first one*, Lexy thought.

Lexy saw Anna roll her eyes at Red Mohawk's comment. She was about to offer a firm response when a pretty Hispanic student wearing a tight shirt that showed her midriff raised her expensively manicured hand and joined the discussion: "First of all, that's totally offensive. And secondly, she can't be sixteen and be enrolled in college."

Jenna Adams smiled triumphantly. "I *am* sixteen! I'm dual enrollment."

Lexy had a poor opinion of dual enrollment students, although she would never confess that to her colleagues. Many DE students were too immature to acclimate to college life. She could tell that Jenna, with her binder filled with pictures of someone Lexy assumed to be her boyfriend and glittery stickers of puppies and flowers, was probably one of those students.

Jenna's lie, as it turned out, was that she had *three* brothers rather than two. How imaginative! Clearly, grading this particular DE student's assignments was going to be exhilarating.

The activity continued in much the same manner, punctuated by occasional interjections by Red Mohawk and another potential class clown: a student, possibly in his early thirties, with a buzz cut. Finally she reached the only familiar name on the roster. She smiled despite herself. "Anna Stevens?"

\* \* \*

Anna cleared her throat. "Okay, here goes. I've been out of school for almost ten years. I jumped out of an airplane on my twenty-fifth birthday, and my dog, Ginger, has been on TV."

She looked up from her paper sheepishly.

"Your dog isn't a TV star!" Red Mohawk guessed.

"Well, not a star exactly, but she has been on the local news. Granted it was just a weather segment, but they filmed us walking around the lake."

Anna wound a strand of hair around her finger in a tight coil. She hated having attention focused on her and would have given anything at that moment for a distraction, like lightning striking outside or a confused bird flying into one of the classroom windows. No such luck. "I've never been skydiving," she admitted, her voice cracking with nervousness and her eyes fixed on the surface of her desk. "I'm afraid of heights."

\* \* \*

*Ten years out of school? That would mean she's in her late twenties...*

Lexy suddenly realized that the students were staring at her, impatience evident in their tight mouths as they waited for her to call the next person on the roster. How long had she been standing there like that? Her face heated slightly as she sought the next name on the list.

Finally, the exercise ended. At two o'clock, fifteen minutes early, she gave the students their assignment for Wednesday and dismissed them. Time for lunch. She began shoveling papers into the worn leather satchel Jules had given her when she secured her first full-time teaching job.

Lexy frowned as she remembered how impatient she had been the morning Jules had surprised her with it. "Honey, I'm late," she'd said, travel mug and lunch bag already in her hands. That was not exactly true. She was the kind of person who was never actually late. When she said she was going to be late, it meant that she wouldn't have the extra twenty minutes in the morning to piddle around before her first class. She used that time to make coffee in her office, return emails, water her plants and make copies if necessary.

"Just a second!" Jules had shouted from the study. Lexy could hear her rummaging through the closet there. They used it for storage so it was chock-full of down coats that they'd never have a use for in Florida, a couple pairs of Rollerblades they'd bought on a whim and used only once, garbage bags full of items she was intending to sell on eBay, although they'd been collecting dust in there for at least a year, and wrapping paper.

"Seriously, I've got to go!"

Jules arrived with the leather bag in her hands. It was decorated with a big red bow. "Now, if you don't like it, don't be polite! I didn't make it, you know."

Lexy had loved it.

She ran her fingers over the initials Jules had had monogrammed on the front flap, her eyes welling up with tears.

A female voice interrupted her reminiscing. "Dr. Strayer?"

"Yes?" Lexy answered without glancing up.

"That vending machine coffee's pretty rancid. You should try The Grind on Central. They have an excellent house latte."

Lexy looked up and was momentarily startled to find Anna's green gaze upon her. Even though she knew it wasn't, the exchange felt sort of…intimate. Immediately she mustered the most professional voice she could. "Thanks. I'll do that."

She pulled her eyes away and busied herself with the task of brushing nonexistent chalk dust from her right pant leg.

"See you Wednesday," Anna said cheerfully as she turned to exit the room.

Lexy exhaled one long breath. *Maybe I* should *go out on Friday*, she thought.

# CHAPTER TWO

Jennifer was reading the posted campus hours on the placard outside Andrea Cole's office when she was startled by a hand on her shoulder.

"Are you the welcome wagon, Professor Gardiner?" Andrea Cole smiled broadly, her crème blouse and dark khaki trousers complementing her impossibly dark eyes and short jet-black hair.

"I am." Jennifer tried to calm her heart, which had leaped at the touch on her shoulder as if Cole had fired the starter pistol at a track meet. "And it's Jennifer." She stepped aside to allow Andrea the room necessary to unlock her office door.

"Not Jen or Jenny?" she asked as she fiddled with the lock.

"I never really liked either of those. Too common."

Jennifer had always hated her name. She found her parents' banality, as evidenced by the names of her brother, Michael, and herself, to be painfully disturbing.

Their marriage seemed passionless too, as if their edges had long ago been worn down to nothing. Jennifer had no memories of them touching, aside from brushing shoulders perhaps when they passed in the hall. She recalled her mother and father sitting at each end of their long dining room table, cutting away at their steak or their bland chicken breast and hardly even glancing at each other unless it was to ask for the salt or the green beans.

Her brother Michael lived in a colonial in Newmarket, New Hampshire, with his Stepford wife and two sets of twins, a consequence of fertility drugs, all with names beginning with B: Brian, Bobby, Beth and Brenda. The proximity of her Portsmouth apartment to her brother's home in Newmarket had made it impossible for Jennifer to bow out of the holiday parties and family get-togethers. Now, with 1,300 miles between them, she was saved from the parties but not from the annual family Christmas photo. The kids' matching red and green jumpsuits always made her gag. Michael had extended not only the family name but also the family motto: *live the most boring, predictable life possible.*

Sixteen years with the same telecommunications company. Sixteen years of steadily chipping away at that iceberg of a mortgage like Sisyphus and his boulder. Sixteen years of having sex with the same woman. The most excitement he saw was refacing the kitchen cabinets or adding prime channels to his cable menu. Jennifer shuddered at the thought. In their last conversation, he had berated her for what he called her "childish and irresponsible lifestyle." "You act like a teenager," he'd said. "All that whoring around in expensive cars that you can't even afford!" She could hear her nieces whining in the background, to which he said a muffled, "Just a minute. Daddy's on the phone." When his full voice returned, clearly directed at her, he shouted, "You never had to even break a sweat for your success!" She could tell he'd slammed the phone down because there was a tinny sound just before the line went dead.

She wasn't childish or irresponsible. She was *free*—free to meet interesting women, some of whom might be as generous with their financial assets as they were with their asses. Michael was a slave—chained to his boulder of *B*'s. And what could he possibly know about hard work, sitting in a cubicle all day? She'd written three books! The only creative energy he exerted at work was in changing his screensaver. No, she refused to allow her life to be anything other than passionate and unpredictable. And who better to be passionate with than Andrea Cole.

"So, Andrea—"

"Andy," the woman said abruptly, turning dark brown eyes in Jennifer's direction as she pushed the door open and gestured her in.

"Andy," Jennifer stammered, caught off guard by the suddenness of the gesture and the low, sultry quality of Andy Cole's voice. Jennifer slid down that voice into her bedroom and imagined Andy Cole stretched out on silk sheets with her back arched and her mouth swollen and wet. *My god!* she thought. *Stop it! Get hold of yourself!*

"I was curious," she choked through a dry throat, "if you might want to go to lunch sometime? I don't think you've met Lexy Strayer yet, but she and I usually go off campus for lunch, and there's a great little deli that opened on Fourth and—"

"I'd love to." The boldness of Andy's stare forced Jennifer to look away. An odd, prickly heat crept up her spine and her palms became clammy. A rush of fear consumed her—a fear that she could be swallowed whole by the sexy darkness she found in Andy Cole's eyes. If she didn't get out from under that stare soon, she might collapse, right there in her office. She gave herself a shake. Usually *she* was the one in charge; she was the tease. *What's happening to me?*

"Well, I'll email you then later this week to make arrangements," she managed as she turned to leave.

* * *

Lexy stared in horror at the image in the mirror. This was the fourth outfit she had tried on and nothing seemed right. The snug Indigo Girls concert T-shirt and vintage stone-washed jeans would have drawn the eye of any female barfly in the 1990s. Now it only caused her to recall with revulsion that moment when, a decade after the *Love Boat* reruns ceased, her mother had descended the stairs in a tube top and clogs hidden beneath drapey bell-bottoms to go on her first post-divorce date. Lexy realized with sudden defeat that the contents of her closet were twenty years older than she felt. It was time to call in the Special Forces.

Rand answered on the second ring. "Hey, Babe. What's up?" he asked. Rand and Ari lived in the condo next door to Lexy's. Rand, a flamboyant and talented pianist for a fine dining restaurant, and Ari, the subdued stereotypical accountant, had been a couple for six years. Their miniature apricot-colored poodle, Princess, who trailed Rand wherever he went, completed the family picture.

"Fashion crisis, Rand. I thought you could help."

"I'll be right over."

Rand always burst through doors as if he were the fire brigade. Although Lexy was accustomed to his melodramatic style of entering places, she was still startled when she heard the door to her condo swing abruptly open, the doorknob hitting the rubber doorstop with a thud and rebounding. Rand had obviously been in the process of bleaching his hair when he was interrupted by Lexy's call for help. She could smell the bleach from a room away. He ran down the hallway, wearing an apron that barely stretched around his ample middle and a shower cap over his white-gooped locks, Princess in an angora sweater and fake diamond collar following at his heels. "I came as soon as I could!" It had been no more than sixty seconds since he had hung up.

Rand took one look at her outfit and his hands shot up to his cheeks. "My God, woman! This *is* an emergency!"

Rand rummaged through her closet and her drawers, clucking at regular intervals and mocking just about everything she owned. Finally he decided on an earthy olive-green tank top and boot cut jeans with a low-heel leather boot.

"I don't know what I would have done without you, Rand," Lexy said as she gazed approvingly at her own reflection. She turned to the side to see her profile.

"You probably would have worn hot pink leg warmers and a *Flashdance* cut sweatshirt," he laughed.

Rand glanced at his watch, and his expression changed to one of alarm. "I've been bleaching for thirty minutes! If I don't get this out, I'll be clogging the shower drain with my precious hair." He scooped Princess up in one sweep of his hand and set her in the crook of his arm. "Good luck on your date or whatever it is you're doing."

"Jennifer's taking me to Hannah B's."

Rand's right eyebrow shot up. "I thought you weren't the bar type?"

"I'm not, but you know how persuasive she can be." Rand had never actually met Jennifer, since Lexy was sure that they would rub each other the wrong way, but she had complained enough about the woman for Rand to know exactly what she meant. Both Rand and Jennifer needed to be the center of attention at all times, and Lexy feared that putting two queens together in one room would make for a very bloody chess game.

"Well, have fun fending off those scary bull dykes. You'll be missing Corporate Queen Night tonight." Every Friday night Rand and Ari had a different themed party. At the last one she had attended—Mexican Fiesta Night—they drank margaritas, wore sombreros, ate nachos and watched a marathon of Antonio Banderas's films. "You can't beat Meryl in *The Devil Wears Prada*," Rand said as he closed the condo door behind him.

Lexy shuddered, imagining how noxious the combined smells of melting popcorn butter and Rand's hair bleach were going to be. Suddenly the prospect of going out seemed less daunting.

\* \* \*

Lexy nervously sipped at her second glass of Shiraz. She was startled by the intercom announcing Jennifer's arrival at the gate.

"Lex Luther, lemme in!" a familiar voice shouted.

She punched in the key code to unlock the south condo gate where Jennifer would pick her up in her new silver BMW M6 convertible. A warmth spread through her veins when she stood. Perhaps she should have stuck to one glass.

As she slid into the convertible, Lexy thought again how unfair it was for one woman to have so many natural advantages. Jennifer's short, reddish-brown, naturally wavy hair was the kind that could be fingered through or tousled and still retain its shape. Her broad shoulders and tall frame projected confidence. She had amazing fashion sense, to boot. Tonight she was wearing a stylish suit that she told Lexy she'd found on the sales rack at Neiman Marcus and a fitted crisp white blouse open far enough to reveal a hint of her silky bra. This, coupled with her smoky, flirtatious gaze, gave her a magnetic appeal.

* * *

When Jennifer pried the door to Hannah B's open, Lexy was immediately assailed by a malodorous cloud of smoke that billowed from the bar as if the door were the mouth of a dragon.

It took her eyes a moment to adjust to the smoky, dimly lit interior. She surveyed the place as Jennifer paid the cover charge to an older hippie-looking woman with dangly earrings and a tortoiseshell necklace.

Two pool tables were positioned to the left of the entrance. The main bar, a traditional thick oak with heavy varnish, was L-shaped and set against the right wall. In the back of the main room was a moderately sized dance floor. It was currently empty while several women, presumably the DJ and Hannah's loyal helpers, conducted sound and light checks. Tables and booths surrounded the dance floor and the pool area, and high swivel stools marked a secondary bar line that bisected the room. Off the dance area was an outside courtyard with another bar and additional seating. The main bar area was relatively crowded; both pool tables were occupied, and most of the tables and booths were filled.

Jennifer placed her hand on Lexy's shoulder to catch her attention and introduce her. "Lexy, this is Eden. Eden, this is my friend and colleague, Lexy Strayer. She teaches English at OCC too."

"Nice to meet you." Lexy took the woman's beringed hand in her own. She could tell instantly that Eden likely ate tofu, listened to Crosby, Stills and Nash and owned a lot of camping gear.

"Eden runs the Dog Wash on Lexington Avenue," Jennifer added. "She's helping Hannah out tonight."

"Hey, if you two aren't busy over Labor Day weekend, my partner, Paige, and I are having a barbecue on that Monday."

"You know me, Eden, this is way too far in advance to commit. I could have a hot date or something." Jennifer laughed. "But Lexy, you should go."

"Are you saying *I* won't have a hot date?"

Lexy felt a nudge from behind as the line of women waiting to get in grew impatient.

"Don't take it personally, Professor; beer is like food for these softball chicks." Eden winked at Lexy and Jennifer. "Here's my card if you decide to come," she said, placing a tan business card with a cute, sudsy sheepdog in a claw-foot tub into Lexy's hand. "The house is right next to the Dog Wash."

As Jennifer guided Lexy into the main room with a hand on her shoulder, eyes from all directions seemed to turn their way. Lexy felt exposed and vulnerable, like in that recurring dream where she walked into a department meeting stark naked and laughter rippled through the conference room like fire in a cornfield during a drought. The dream usually ended with Lexy futilely trying to cover her privates and her breasts with the small yellow legal pad she had in her hands.

Jennifer, as if sensing her companion's alarm, hooked her arm around Lexy's and led her in the direction of the main bar. "First, a drink." She took a closer look at Lexy's expression. "On second thought, let's make that a shot."

As Jennifer conversed with the bartender, a spiky-haired girl with multiple piercings and a tribal tattoo on the side of her neck, Lexy couldn't help but think how painful getting them must have been. She was a wimp when it came to pain. She remembered when a friend had convinced her in college to get her belly button pierced. Steph had gone first. When the Harley-looking guy in surgical gloves pushed what appeared to be a thick fish hook through Steph's pinched flesh, Lexy had instantly passed out. Needless to say, she remained unpierced and free of tattoos to this day.

"Two Jager Bombs then," Jennifer said as she pushed a crisp twenty toward the bartender.

The girl emptied the contents of the green liquor bottle into a brushed metal shaker and yelled over her shoulder as she lined up two shot glasses on the counter, "Yo, Anna, we're outta Jager! Can you grab one from the back?"

Lexy casually glanced at the women that surrounded the bar. It was a mixed crowd. A heavyset woman with closely cropped salt-and-pepper hair sat to their right, looking despondent as she picked at the label of her beer. Two ultra-feminine women sporting dark lipstick that made Lexy think of Elvira were chatting in a conspiratorial manner and watching the pool game across from them. One of them, noticing Lexy's eyes on her, smiled and winked. Lexy immediately looked away, wondering, probably for the fifth time since they'd arrived, how she'd let Jennifer convince her to go out. This so wasn't her scene.

Lexy's attention was brought back to the hustle and bustle behind the bar when she heard a familiar voice say, "Here you go, Trish."

"Thanks, Gorgeous."

It was Anna—her Anna, that is, her *student* Anna—handing a full bottle of Jager to the brunette serving them. Lexy, shocked, gulped and stared at the woman before her. Anna's hair was pulled back in a loose ponytail, leaving her shoulders and slender neck bare above a flattering black tank top that hugged her breasts and clung to her flat stomach. Lexy's eyes slid from Anna's neck down to her chest before a last shred of professionalism forced them back up to her face. Anna's nonplussed eyes met hers there, and Lexy immediately reddened and swallowed hard.

"Dr. Strayer?" Anna's voice quivered a bit.

Lexy, desperately trying to think of something appropriate to say, stood there in a stupor, her lips slightly parted.

Jennifer thrust a hand in Anna's direction. "My friend here clearly has no manners. I'm Jennifer Gardiner."

Anna wiped her palm on the bistro apron at her waist. "Anna Stevens," she said quietly as she took Jennifer's outstretched hand in her own.

"Dr. Strayer's name is Lexy on the weekends, by the way."

Lexy watched Jennifer's lips curl into a seductive smile. She gritted her teeth and forced her thoughts away from where that smile might be intended to lead her student.

"Nice to meet you," Anna said. After one quick glance at Lexy, she made a fast retreat to the back room out of which she had come.

"Bottoms up!" Jennifer clinked Lexy's glass with her own.

Lexy downed the contents of her drink in three large swallows as if it were water, shuddering before setting the glass down hard on the bar.

Jennifer watched, mouth agape. "Well, that's unusual for you. Trying to put out a fire?"

"That was one of my students!"

"So? It's not like you're in the closet."

It's true that she wasn't in the closet. She didn't advertise her sexuality on campus, but she didn't lie about it either. Not anymore.

Just the other day, for example, Lexy had been forced into conversation with Jean Marie Belkin, a new adjunct in the speech department. She had been washing her hands in the lavatory as Jean Marie emerged from one of the stalls. When Jean Marie asked innocently how Lexy's weekend had been, she'd told her she had gotten a lot done—she'd washed her car, finished grading a stack of essays and sorted through her closet for items she wanted to give to Goodwill.

"You should have your boyfriend clean your car!" Jean Marie said, laughing. "Those car waxes are terrible on the manicure."

Lexy had smiled her standard nervous smile, the one with no teeth showing and her lips in almost a completely flat line aside from the raised corners. "I don't have a boyfriend," she said. "I'm a lesbian."

The syllables always felt uncomfortable in her mouth, as if it were a foreign word that she was sure she was mispronouncing. And, as with each time she was forced to say it, she had to watch as the listener's face transformed into that look of confusion and horror mixed with forced pleasantries and politeness that she knew so well. Poor Jean Marie. She was the kind of woman who listened to taped sermons in the car on her ride to campus, the kind of woman who knew what doilies were for. And she clearly hadn't known what was coming. She was now desperately looking for a way to get out of the bathroom without appearing rude. Lexy had taken pity on her, exiting the restroom herself. She could swear she heard the woman sigh in relief.

Had it not been for Jules, the conversation with Jean Marie would have ended with the nervous smile. In fact, prior to Jules convincing Lexy to come out of the closet at work, she might have even appeared to agree with Jean Marie: "Yes, I *should* have him do it." Jules, being fearless herself, had argued that if Lexy wasn't proud of who she was then she certainly couldn't expect others to be.

"Why are you having a nervous breakdown?" Jennifer asked in an accusatory tone. "It's no biggie! This generation could care less about who's gay. *Really*."

"Can we get out of here?" Lexy rubbed at her smoke-irritated eyes. Jennifer didn't get it. It wasn't the fact that a student would realize that she was gay that was making her uncomfortable. It was the fact that she now knew that Anna was gay and that Anna now knew she was gay. Lexy's stomach threatened upheaval and she swallowed hard.

"Don't be silly." Jennifer patted her knee. "Look around, Lex. There are beautiful women here and the night just started!" She surveyed the room like a hungry wolf.

"Fine, but I need another drink." Lexy motioned to the tattooed bartender.

* * *

Anna paced back and forth in the storage room, trying to control her breathing. *Lexy*, she thought. *Lexy Strayer.* The name sounded European and mysterious to her, like the name of a character in a romantic thriller.

Marie, who had been unloading some bottles on the shelf, asked, "What the hell got into you?"

"My literature professor is here," Anna said, plopping her body down like a rag doll in one of the folding chairs next to a storage bin of cocktail napkins and toothpicks.

"And?" Marie pushed a box out of the way with her elbow to make more room on the shelf.

"And...nothing, I guess." Anna considered telling Marie about her attraction to her professor but then thought that she might sound pathetically young and immature. Marie was also not the kind to talk about emotions. In fact, it was rare for Marie to extend the effort necessary to sustain a conversation. She might contribute two or three sentences, but rarely were those sentences designed to elicit a response.

Marie eyed Anna suspiciously for a moment before returning her attention to the boxes and crates. "Well, it's pretty busy out there. So, if you could speed up your little meltdown, I'm sure Trish and Lana would appreciate it."

* * *

Jennifer glanced at Lexy. "Are you determined to have a terrible time?"

"What? No." Lexy smiled weakly. "I'm having fun."

Jennifer laughed. "That's so convincing." Her eyes scanned the tables. "Oh, hey, there's someone I want to introduce you to," she said, linking arms with Lexy.

Charlie's real name was Charlize, Jennifer explained quickly as they walked over, although she wouldn't hesitate to deck anyone who called her that. She was sitting with her girlfriend of eight years, Rachel.

Charlie and Rachel were the stereotypical lesbian couple, Lexy learned. Although they had distinctly different body types, they often dressed in each other's clothes. In fact, it was common to see Rachel wearing cargo pants with the bottoms rolled up since she was the shorter of the two. They sported identical hairstyles, the short *Ellen* sitcom cut that tried for edgy but failed without the right hair product, and they even had the same mannerisms and speech patterns. Jennifer said she never could tell which one answered the phone when she called their apartment.

Lexy warmed to the couple almost immediately, although Charlie smacked Lexy's back a little too hard in greeting and Rachel almost burned her when she shook hands while holding a cigarette precariously between her index and middle fingers.

"I don't know why you smoke those things," Charlie grumbled, motioning with her eyes to Rachel's cigarette pack.

"I don't know how you can drink that crap," Rachel retorted with a sly grin as she eyed Charlie's Budweiser.

The couple bickered constantly, but Lexy found them both entertaining and endearing, like Marie and Frank on *Everybody Loves Raymond*. She heard all about their three furry children: Pipsqueak, a small rat terrier; Bubbles, a sheepdog, who was named by Charlie's nephew after a painful mishap with a bubble wand; and Mozart, a dachshund. They even broke out wallet-sized photos of their "kids."

Lexy grew bored, though, when Charlie began to discuss her work. She owned a pool-cleaning business, which is how she knew Jennifer—she maintained the kidney-shaped pool at Jennifer's house. Fortunately, the discussion of chemical treatments didn't last long enough to warrant a yawn.

Much more interesting was Rachel, who managed a local bookstore, called Words of Worth, on Mills Avenue. Lexy had shopped there a few times, but she didn't recall having seen her there. Their window feature this month, she was telling Jennifer, was Jennifer's book *Death by Dismemberment*. Jennifer had written three murder mysteries now under the name J.

Deveaux. They had been published by a small local company called Flemming Press.

Lexy had read only *Icy Waters*, the first in the series and set in New England. She'd found it a bit on the pulpy and predictable side for her taste. She'd read the back of the other two so that she could at least pretend to have read them in conversation with Jennifer. She suspected that her friend used her publication credits as another ploy, like her expensive TAG Heuer watch and her BMW convertible, to attract more dates. Jennifer's spending habits, which were far too lavish for their college salaries or her book royalties, had made Lexy wonder if she came from money, but any mention of her upbringing seemed utterly unimpressive—a standard middle-class household. And her many inquiries had ended with what Lexy assumed to be a deliberate change of subject.

"What do you think of the cover of this one?" Jennifer asked them.

Lexy didn't like it. It had the kitsch of all those popular television crime dramas. A half-opened body bag lay on the wood floor, which was splattered dramatically with blood. Strands of long hair, darkened a deep crimson, escaped through the zipper. Most of the woman's face was obscured, except for a single blue eye that stared vacantly at the reader through a slit in the bag. The best part was the solitary severed leg that lay just to the right of the bag on the floor in a pool of blood as if it had escaped the coroner's attention.

"Well, it's definitely creepy," Lexy said.

"You think that's creepy? You should've seen the first version!" Jennifer laughed. "It had the detectives crouching down to inspect the naked, bloody body parts."

"That doesn't sound so bad," Charlie said.

"Yeah, except for their faces—at least the lead detective. She was staring at a severed torso with a sultry, turned-on look."

Lexy gasped in revulsion.

"The cover artist was a real sicko."

"Apparently."

"I got his ass fired. And I swear if that prick calls me one more time, I'll have him arrested."

"You got him hired?" Rachel asked.

"Fired, I said 'got him *fired*.'"

"Let's go somewhere else," Rachel said. "I can barely hear you over that pulsing bass."

The women moved to the courtyard to continue their conversation.

\* \* \*

Anna watched Dr. Strayer, Jennifer and two women she recognized as regulars, armed with fresh drinks, make their way out to the courtyard. As she mixed a Long Island Ice Tea for a young woman with a small gold eyebrow ring, she took a few moments to study her professor. She looked sexy with her hair down instead of braided. Looking at her now, it was easy for Anna to imagine running her fingers through that hair and even grabbing a fistful of it as she kissed her hard.

Were Jennifer and Lexy together? She saw Jennifer's eyes scanning the room in an almost predatory manner and quickly dismissed the idea.

\* \* \*

Lexy, buzzed from the Jager and the wine she had earlier, watched the dancers and nursed a diet soda as she half-listened to Jennifer flirt with the pretty blond bartender and Charlie and Rachel argue about who was responsible for losing their Tupperware lids.

Lexy's eyes fell on one particularly attractive couple on the dance floor. As they languidly moved to the music, a handsome woman with a boyish haircut parted her pretty brunette dance partner's legs with her knee, pushed some of the brunette's long hair aside and kissed her exposed neck. Lexy watched her left hand creep slowly from the small of the woman's back to the top of her buttocks—then, feeling like a voyeur, she turned and watched the women gathered at the inside bar instead.

The bar was busy, with a line of women waiting to be served and the bartenders in constant motion. As Lexy watched, one of Anna's toned arms stretched upward to reach for a bottle on the top shelf. Shortly afterward, the young woman wiped her forehead with the back of her hand. Lexy imagined what she would look like working out at the gym—wet with perspiration, the toned muscles of her arms, legs and stomach flexing under the strain. She flushed, ashamed of the prurient thoughts running through her mind, afraid someone would catch her ogling Anna. As she struggled to turn her thoughts down more acceptable paths—adding clay to the armature wire to flesh out the curve of a hip, the swell of a breast—someone did catch her: Anna, turning toward the courtyard to serve another customer. Their eyes met and for just a moment there was a connection, a confirmation of mutual interest, mutual attraction. Anna smiled in response, and Lexy immediately looked away. Instead of those beautiful emerald eyes, she became an unwilling witness to Jennifer's latest seduction.

The bartender Jennifer was flirting with had a petite nose and cheeks slightly dusted with sun freckles. She was probably more than ten years younger than Jennifer—who was, like Lexy, in her midthirties. In spite of the piercing in her nose, something about her made Lexy think of wholesomeness, apple pie and hopscotch. The one playing games here, though, was her friend. She was saddened by the thought that Jennifer was likely going to whisk the innocent young woman off her feet, have a night of mad passionate sex with her and then make up some excuse to leave before the sun came up.

Lexy nudged Charlie and asked quietly where the bathroom was. Charlie pointed toward the pool table area, and she excused herself. By the time Lexy reached the restroom, she had to go pretty badly. She pushed the door open hurriedly—and almost collided with Anna.

"Sorry!"

"Dr. Strayer, I'm sorry. I didn't see you."

"Please, I almost ran you over." Suddenly, getting into a bathroom stall wasn't quite as urgent as staring into Anna's eyes again. Lexy's heart began to race. The fact that they were so close to each other in the doorway, neither making any attempt to move, combined with the buzz from the alcohol made her forget herself, her position and the college completely. For a moment she thought she might lean in and kiss her. Anna appeared to be thinking something similar.

"It's Lexy." She'd meant to sound nonchalant, but what came out of her sounded, even to Lexy, more like a purr, impossibly sexy and feline. Anna's body responded accordingly, closing the space between the two of them.

Lexy, seeing Anna lean toward her, instinctively took a step backward. She would have continued retreating had she not been stopped by the door. The contact restored a degree of self-control. Cursing herself, she worked to dispel the feeling of attraction by silently repeating the mantra, "*She's your student, damn it. Your student!*"

Anna stepped back too, evidently seeing something in Lexy's face that told her the tides had changed. "Lexy's a pretty name," she said with the lopsided, dimpled smile that Lexy remembered seeing the day they had met at the vending machine.

Lexy quickly squeezed past her and into one of the stalls. She latched the door and tried to calm her breathing. Through the crack between the stall door and its frame, she watched Anna's reflection in the wall mirror. Anna was still smiling as she pushed the door open with an open palm and left.

*Fuck!* Lexy thought. *Fuck, fuck, fuck!*

# CHAPTER THREE

Jennifer had arranged for Lexy, Andy Cole and herself to meet at the new deli for lunch on Tuesday afternoon. She and Lexy, having driven there together in her BMW, arrived first.

"I hope this place is fast," Lexy said as she removed her sunglasses and set them down on the linen tablecloth. "I'm already behind in my grading." Just the thought of the stack of freshman comparison and contrast essays waiting for her in her office was enough to ignite a headache behind her left eye. *Why didn't I study something I could grade with a Scantron machine?* she wondered.

Jennifer unfolded her menu. "All work and no play makes Lexy a mean girl."

"Speaking of play, what happened with you and the blonde after you dropped me off Friday night?"

"We played mah-jong and then I took her home, of course." Jennifer's eyes were drawn to the woman speaking to the hostess. "Here she is." Jennifer nudged Lexy's elbow. "God, she's sexy!" she whispered.

Lexy took in the tall figure before her. Andy Cole was certainly as dark and handsome as Jennifer had described her. She had tan skin, strong features and broad shoulders, the muscles of which were easily discernible in the Oxford polo she wore. In fact, if seen from behind, Lexy would probably mistake her for a man. She looked like she could break Jennifer in two like a twig.

"Andy Cole, meet my oldest friend at OCC, Lexy Strayer."

Andy Cole's hand felt large and consuming, Lexy thought. She resisted the impulse to try to wriggle out of the grasp as quickly as she could. The woman was an Amazon. "Finally, I get to meet the mysterious new addition to the department," she said, smiling despite the crushing handshake.

"Mysterious?" Andy's dark eyebrows rose as she sat in the only empty chair at their table.

"Well, yeah, usually there's quite a bit of gossip-sharing when a new person is hired, even on temporary contract," Jennifer said, "and no one seemed to know anything about you. In fact, you were a bit of a surprise." Jennifer laid her hand on top of Andy's. "A nice surprise though," she added.

"Well, Professor Belman's sabbatical was sort of a last-minute decision, I hear." Andy pulled her hand out from under Jennifer's, opened her menu and changed the subject: "So, what's good?"

"I hear their homemade soup is an orgasm in a bread bowl." Jennifer was quite shamelessly undressing Andy Cole with her eyes. It was fortunate, Lexy thought, that Andy's attention was absorbed by the menu. Lexy kicked her friend under the table.

"What?" Jennifer rubbed her shin.

Lexy gave her the disapproving eyebrow crunch, the imperious stare that her own mother had perfected to discipline her on occasions when she was in the presence of company she was trying to impress.

Jennifer rolled her eyes in response.

"So, Andy, where did you teach before OCC?" Lexy asked.

"Uh…" Andy shifted in her seat, bumping her plate and causing her silverware to clank noisily with the movement. "This is actually my first teaching gig."

Jennifer and Lexy exchanged surprised glances. People generally weren't hired on four-month contract without prior teaching experience.

"Well, I mean, my first *full-time* teaching position," Andy corrected. "I taught as an adjunct at Southern New Hampshire University."

Jennifer clapped her hands excitedly. "A fellow New Englander! Lex is from Maine and I'm from Portsmouth, New Hampshire."

"I grew up in South Carolina, and moved to Manchester when I joined the…" Andy paused briefly, seeming to collect her thoughts, "teaching profession. I spent a little time in Virginia and then, of course, moved here."

Lexy hated this sort of chit-chatty, getting-to-know-you banter, but they hadn't even ordered yet and bouts of silence were equally insufferable to her. "And how was your first week at OCC?" she asked, even though she really wasn't all that interested.

"Good, thanks to the welcome wagon here." Andy smiled warmly at Jennifer.

They chatted about their classes. Newer faculty were saddled with the least coveted freshman survey courses—in their department that was composition. Andy had five freshman composition classes, at which both women flinched.

"Not even one lit class?" Jennifer asked sympathetically.

"I studied rhetoric, so composition's really my expertise," she explained. "My thesis was on the Bartholomae and Elbow debate."

Jennifer's laugh was cut short by Andy's scowl. "What, you're serious?" Jennifer blinked. "Sorry, I just…I took a couple of composition pedagogy classes in grad school and…well, maybe I didn't have the right teachers."

"Maybe not."

Conversation veered to their offices and the fact that only Jennifer was blessed with a window. Lexy suspected that this was due to the fact that she had slept with Sandra Gutierrez, the chair of the planning committee.

Lexy gave Andy plant advice, not that she was a green thumb, but she knew through trial and error that offices without windows could support only cacti and bamboo.

The waiter arrived and took down their orders. "Something from the bar?" he asked Andy.

"I don't drink." There was a practiced finality to her statement that made Lexy wonder if she was a recovering alcoholic. She continued to study the woman as she passed her menu back to the waiter. Perhaps Jennifer was right. She certainly did look the part. In fact, she really couldn't be more of a lesbian unless she had driven a motorcycle to the restaurant.

"Did you have trouble finding a parking spot?" Lexy asked.

"Nope, not with my new Speedmaster," Andy said proudly.

"A motorcycle?" Lexy almost laughed out loud.

"Not just a motorcycle, a *Triumph Speedmaster.*"

Jennifer's eyes opened wide. "I'd love to go for a ride sometime!" she blurted. "I mean, if you wouldn't mind a passenger."

"I'd give you a ride back to campus today, but I only brought the one helmet."

A helmet wasn't required for the kind of riding that Jennifer wanted to do, Lexy thought, mentally shaking her head. It was clear that she was totally head over heels in lust.

\* \* \*

"So, 'Ms. Deveaux,' I'm a big fan. I've read all of your books." Andy desperately hoped that this was the right time to bring up the subject. At Jennifer's surprised expression, she added, "The department secretary might've let it slip."

"You really like them?" Jennifer batted long eyelashes painted black with mascara in Andy's direction.

"I love them! Where do you get the inspiration for your characters? They're really well drawn."

"Well, actually, the victims are fashioned after ex-girlfriends. You know what they say: write what you know."

The ex-girlfriend connection wasn't news to Andy. That's why she was here, after all, because of Mona and Teresa. But she needed a window into the conversation.

"So Izzy from your newest book, is she based on someone you dated?"

"My most recent ex, Samantha, left me for her *male* yoga instructor; hence, the grotesque dismemberment." Jennifer smiled, showing perfectly straight and white teeth. "Revenge is a dish best served cold, as they say."

Andy felt sick, remembering Mona Feldtman, washed up in York Beach, Maine, her hands and feet bound with electrical tape and her skin blue and bloated from being long submerged in the icy waters of the Atlantic Ocean.

"You okay?" Jennifer asked.

Andy mentally shook herself, remembering where she was. "Of course." She smiled.

\* \* \*

"You have to remember," Lexy said as she sat on the edge of her desk, "at only fifteen O'Connor watched her father die of lupus and knew that she was likely facing her own death when she herself was diagnosed with the disease." Lexy crossed her legs. "So religious salvation became a primary focus in her writing." Although she was normally at ease in front of a classroom of students, with Anna's eyes on her she felt disconcerted and somewhat vulnerable.

"So, who's saved in this story?" a male surfer-looking student with dirty blond, shoulder-length hair and a graphic T-shirt asked. The back of his hair jutted out from his scalp in all sorts of unnatural angles, giving the impression that he had rolled out of bed and come directly to class. She hoped he had at least brushed his teeth.

"Well, let's look at the details. After the grandmother, who up to this point has proven herself to be deceitful, manipulative, racist and generally annoying, hears the Misfit's voice crack, she reaches out to him, in what many critics assume to be her only compassionate move in the entire story. And it's at that point that he shoots her three times in the chest. Why three?"

Anna removed the blue pen cap from her mouth and offered, "Because it has religious significance?"

Lexy smiled approvingly. "Yes! Three wise men, the trinity, the three days it took Christ to resurrect, the three times Peter denied Christ. It's no coincidence that there are also three men in the hearse-like automobile—the Misfit and his two cohorts. And when we see the grandmother again, she's sitting like an innocent child and smiling up at a cloudless sky…"

* * *

As Anna listened intently, she felt a heat wash through her body. Part of it was the excitement of being in the classroom again, of tackling interesting topics. But mostly it was Lexy, she had to admit, watching the slight rise and fall of Lexy's chest through the opening of her blouse as she spoke.

"Just like in 'Revelation,' our main character experiences an epiphany because of a horrifically terrifying experience, which is what ultimately allows her to receive God's grace, at least in O'Connor's view." Lexy glanced at the wall clock and promptly closed the thick anthology that was open in her lap. "Okay, folks, don't forget your blue books for the in-class essay on Monday."

As Lexy erased the board, Anna lingered, packing up her things as slowly as she could. Finally gathering her courage, she said, "Interesting class today, Dr. Strayer." She had grappled with the idea of calling her Lexy but decided against it.

Lexy swung around, her grip closing tightly on the eraser. "Well, Flannery O'Connor is pretty fascinating," she said in what was obviously intended to be a professional tone.

Anna suddenly felt foolish for having approached this accomplished and beautiful woman. She stared mutely at Lexy over the rows of desks between them.

"Well," Lexy turned her attention back to the blackboard, "have a good rest of the week then."

"You too," Anna said in defeat.

\* \* \*

While Patrick Reilly, Andy's partner at the FBI field office in Tampa, developed a list of Samanthas in the Orange County area who might have had relations with Jennifer, she called the task force investigators in the homicide units in York and Portsmouth to get her weekly updates and fill them in on what she'd learned from the suspect.

She had just hung up with James Cormier, a homicide detective in York, when she heard a knock at her office door. Having not had time yet to put construction paper or comic strips over the long vertical plate of clear glass in her door like the other instructors in her hallway, she could see Jennifer Gardiner's dark lipsticked lips curl into a sexy smile as she turned to answer the knock. Why did she have to be so damn attractive? Andy wondered as she opened the door and beckoned the author in, a phony smile of her own plastered on her face.

"To what do I owe the pleasure, Professor Gardiner?"

"I was wondering if you might have that extra helmet today, because I'm looking for a ride home."

Bold, Andy thought, somewhat impressed.

"I got a lift this morning with Lexy," Jennifer continued, "and she's staying late to grade."

"Actually, I didn't ride the bike today; I drove the Jeep. More room," she said, indicating with her eyes the two crates of books and office supplies that rested on the floor between them. An extremely thick, weathered-looking hardcover with *The Complete Works of Shakespeare* on the binding in gold leaf lettering seemed to catch Jennifer's eye.

"What's your favorite play?"

"*Macbeth*. I like the guilt factor myself, bloodied hands and all." Andy watched her closely, gauging her reaction.

"The corruption of power and one of the strongest female characters in literary history—very compelling."

Andy couldn't detect any change in Jennifer's jovial demeanor. "I'd be happy to give you a ride in the Jeep," she said.

"Great!" Jennifer chirped.

As Jennifer climbed into the army green Jeep Liberty Renegade complete with fog lights and bike rack, Andy surreptitiously slid the file folder that had been resting on the driver's-side floor mat under the seat with her foot. If she was going to be spending more time with Jennifer, as she hoped, she'd have to be more careful with such things, she reminded herself.

"Chris Pureka, I *love* her," Jennifer said as she picked up a number of CD cases off the central console. "k.d. lang, not so much."

"Well, pick something and pop it in."

As Jennifer cycled through the songs on Ingrid Michaelson's *Lights Out*, they drove through the neighborhoods surrounding the college, which were dotted with low-hanging oak and maple trees and traditional Florida block homes. Jennifer's home, however, was a two-story Spanish-style house with stucco walls and a red clay-tiled roof. It stood out among the '50s-style houses in the area. The landscaping looked new but tasteful and full of color with a water feature and a brick-paved walkway.

"Home sweet home," Jennifer said as they pulled into the driveway. "How about a cup of cappuccino? I've got a machine that's lucky if it's unboxed once a year."

"Sure," Andy said, shutting off the engine.

As she followed Jennifer to the side entrance, Andy stole a glance through the small rectangular windows in the garage door. The space was empty, as she suspected.

* * *

As Andy sipped her cappuccino, Jennifer noticed how the sunlight filtering through the blinds cast bright bars across the woman's cheek and made her earrings sparkle. "Hey, cool. You and I have the same earrings." She touched one of Andy's half-carat diamond studs with her index finger. "Are they real?" Although Jennifer's certainly looked real, hers were man-made Moissanite diamonds. She chose those because she'd read that even accomplished appraisers were unable to distinguish the cheaper Moissanite from quality diamonds.

"Yes." Andy smiled, tugging on her earlobe. "These were a present to myself when I finished at The Citadel."

"In Charleston?" Jennifer was confused. "Isn't that a military academy?"

"Some of the students are civilians," Andy said after a brief pause. She took another sip of her foamy drink.

"Well, you must be very disciplined then," Jennifer said suggestively, eyeing the tall dark woman's profile.

"That I am."

Jennifer wet her lips, her blue eyes boring into Andy's brown ones. "I *like* disciplined."

# CHAPTER FOUR

On Wednesday night, Anna wiped down the counter of the bar, clearing it of the latest batch of spills. She had hoped that Lexy would return to Hannah B's again. They'd seen each other in class, of course, twice since their Friday night encounter. Their in-class exchanges since then had been stilted and it was clear that if Lexy was going to allow Anna to know her better, that would not happen at the college. Anna hoped for more, but at the very least she'd like to clear the air. It looked like she wasn't going to have the chance.

Around ten thirty, however, she spied Lexy's friend Jennifer chatting with the bouncer. She was so excited that she almost waved at the woman. Jennifer saw her anyway and started making her way over, stopping intermittently to flirt with someone.

"Anna, right?" Jennifer's voice had a glint of a flirtatious Demi Moore raspiness, something she'd undoubtedly been complimented on countless times. Her voice had no effect however, on Anna, whose eyes were busily searching the sea of women behind her for a certain face.

"Yeah, hi again." Anna placed a red cocktail napkin on the counter in front of Jennifer. Might as well just ask, she thought. "Is Dr. Strayer with you tonight?"

"No, Lexy's not really the bar type. She's probably grading your paper. That woman's always working!"

"So what can I get you?"

Jennifer ordered a dirty martini with extra olives. It was clear she had already been drinking. Her speech was slightly slurred, and her eyes were glossy and unfocused.

"Top shelf?"

"Of course." In the mirror behind the bar, Anna saw Jennifer's eyes follow as she stretched her torso to reach the highest shelf and how she licked her lips in response when her shirt rode up slightly. She couldn't say she was flattered, though if the eyes watching her had been Lexy's...

"How 'bout I buy *you* a drink?" Jennifer asked.

"No, thanks. Got a test tomorrow that I need to be sharp for."

"Just one?" Jennifer pouted. The slight edge to her tone indicated that she really was perturbed by Anna's refusal. Anna knew the type well, after ten years of tending bar. It was rare, probably, that Jennifer had to beg for what she wanted. In fact, Anna bet, people usually begged her.

"I really shouldn't, but..." Anna smiled as she speared three olives with a toothpick and plopped them into the full martini glass. "I do have a fifteen-minute break coming up." She could use the time to try to pry information out of Jennifer about Lexy.

Jennifer responded by pulling an olive slowly and seductively off the toothpick with her lips, her eyes fastened on Anna. *This could be trouble*, Anna thought. She poured a little Captain Morgan's Spiced Rum into her Pepsi and joined Jennifer on the other side of the bar. "Thanks for this," she said, raising her glass slightly.

"Thanks for joining me." Jennifer's pale blue eyes unabashedly ran down Anna's neck to her chest and on to her hips, making her uncomfortable. "You have gorgeous green eyes," she said, returning her attention to Anna's face.

Anna rolled her napkin nervously between her thumb and forefinger. Somehow Jennifer's comment didn't feel like a compliment the way she had said it. "So, how long have you and Dr. Strayer known each other?"

"How 'bout a dance?" Jennifer said, acting as if she hadn't heard her.

"I'm not much of a dancer. I—" Anna stammered as Jennifer took hold of her hand. Before she had a chance to protest further, the older woman was leading her by the arm to the dance floor and pulling her body close with strong hands. The impact temporarily shocked her into silence. Before she had regained enough composure to speak out in protest, she was stunned into silence again. Lexy Strayer was standing at the edge of the dance floor. Her brown eyes, big and round, were riveted on them.

Anna pulled out of Jennifer's grasp, muttering a quick apology as she tried to weave through the crowd to reach Lexy. By the time she made it to where she had been standing, however, Lexy was gone.

* * *

Jennifer couldn't believe the girl had left her standing there on the dance floor. She felt utterly humiliated as the women that surrounded them, alerted by Anna's fast retreat, turned to stare at her. *How dare she!* She considered writing Anna into her next book and imagined various torturous scenarios. She hadn't had a poisoning yet. Martinis might be just classy enough for what she had in mind.

* * *

"What the hell?"

Jennifer was befuddled by Arnold Flemming's reaction to her invitation to lunch the next day. She had drafted the first chapter of her new book, tentatively titled *Deadly Martini*, and had called to arrange their usual meeting. To which Arnold had responded curtly with, "Why don't you just send it to the office? I'll look over it and call you to discuss edits."

Something was off. She and Arnold *always* discussed her new plotline and characters at their favorite Japanese restaurant over a sushi boat and a side of edamame. In the past Arnold had looked forward to these sake-filled luncheons so much so that she could barely put him off long enough to write the damn things.

"What's up, Arnold? We always have lunch," she protested.

"Fine," he said, sounding annoyed. "Where do you wanna meet then?"

Jennifer increased the volume on her cell, thinking she must not have heard him correctly. "What?" she asked.

"What restaurant?" Arnold demanded gruffly.

"Where we always meet—Sayako's on Fifth. What the hell's wrong with you, Arnold?"

"Nothing." Arnold sniffled and coughed, sounding very much like the unconvincing voice mails her students left her when they were making excuses for missing work or classes. "Just coming down with something," he said.

"Around two o'clock then?"

"Fine. I'll see you there." With that, Arnold hung up. That was odd too. Since his cruise to Venice four years before, he had ended every phone conversation with her with an enthusiastic "*Ciao*, darling!" It looked like she had a mystery to solve as well as one to write.

* * *

Recognizing the number from the Tampa field office, Andy answered her cell on the first ring. "Agent Cole."

"I've got your Samantha," her partner said in response. "Both Samantha Jensen and Jennifer Gardiner's names were on a lease in Orlando three years ago."

"Did you find a current address for this Samantha?"

"She's not listed, but we traced her to Key West. We suspect that she's living with a guy named John Creighton, the super at the Blue Parrot Apartment Complex there."

"Good work," Andy said. "What else you got for me?"

"The coroner reported that the Portsmouth girl died of smoke inhalation. The fire's been ruled a homicide, but it was a clean job, no prints." The cover of J. Deveaux's second book had featured flames wrapped around the sign advertising the Weeping Willow Bed and Breakfast.

"All right, thanks, Reilly. Call me if you guys find any more leads." Andy sat back in her chair, eyeing the cover of *Death by Dismemberment*, and thought, *I have got to work faster*.

* * *

Jennifer could hear Andy Cole's deskjet printer whirring into action as she reached her office door. "Hey, good looking," she said, leaning her shoulder into the doorframe and pushing some fallen bangs out of her eyes. She was emboldened after the somewhat flirtatious conversation they'd had over cappuccino the other day.

Andy did not look up as she gathered what looked to be Mapquest directions out of the docking bay of her printer.

"You're gonna give a girl a complex, ignoring me like that," Jennifer said.

At that, Andy turned toward her. Jennifer was startled by the irritation she found in her normally welcoming eyes. Without the broad, friendly smile that had become a signature of hers, Andy asked, "What's up? I'm kind of busy."

"Well, I'm off now to meet with my publisher for sushi, but I thought maybe if you weren't doing anything for dinner, we could—"

"Look, I'm sorry, Jennifer, but I've got plans all weekend," Andy interrupted as she began pushing a notepad into a leather backpack.

"Oh." Jennifer tried to keep the disappointment and anger from her voice. "Okay, well, I'll see ya after Labor Day then." With that, she turned and left the office.

* * *

On the way home from lunch with Arnold, Jennifer phoned Lexy. She expected to get her voice mail since she had already left five messages. On the third ring, however, the call was answered.

"Hello?"

"Lex? Where've you been? And why haven't you returned any of my calls?"

"Just busy with papers. What's up?" Lexy's voice sounded uncharacteristically tired and distracted.

"Well, I'm having the weirdest couple of days. I met with Arnold today at Sayako's and I'm telling you, Lex, he looked like himself but it was like *Invasion of the Body Snatchers*. He didn't seem to know anything about my recurring characters, and he ordered a tempura dish. Cooked sushi, *can you imagine?* And his fingernails looked manicured!"

"So? Guys have manicures."

"Yeah, well, not Arnold. And I stopped by Andy's office today before my lunch date just to chat, and she was totally disinterested in me. I mean, she's been drooling over me for weeks, and suddenly, without warning, she practically slams the door in my face. To top it all off, last night at Hannah B's, I flirted with that cute student of yours and she acted as if I had some contagious disease."

"Look, do you need something, Jennifer?" Lexy replied coldly. "Because I'm kinda busy."

"I don't know what's up with people today!" Jennifer shouted. "But you're just the icing on the fucking cake!" She threw her cell at the passenger-side window. *They'll be sorry*, she thought.

* * *

Lexy's head pounded. She shouldn't have gone to Hannah B's last night. It was stupid. Impulsive. And seeing them together—dancing like that... She gritted her teeth. "Jennifer doesn't need to have her hands in *every* woman's pants!" she mumbled angrily to herself. She knew that she had no right to be mad. It wasn't like Anna belonged to her. But the thought of them together—it was just so repulsive! Anna didn't seem to Lexy to be the kind of woman who would be interested in sexual encounters with strangers, so she was angry with Jennifer over what she could potentially do to her. *She could hurt her.*

# CHAPTER FIVE

As Lexy was climbing the steps at the Orange County Community Center that evening for her Thursday night sculpture class, strong fingers closed on her forearm. After a slight start, she pressed the pause button on her iPod and unplugged her ears with a quick yank on the wires.

"Lex! How've you been?" It was Carol, a chunky, gray-haired woman who always functioned at five levels of energy above the average person.

"Great, Carol," Lexy responded. "I've been looking forward to some relaxing clay time."

"Me too! See you inside!" Carol practically bounced her way up the remaining cement steps. Lexy couldn't help but be irritated at how happy the woman always was. She knew it was wrong to feel that way, but she was increasingly angry that her life had turned out the way that it did. Sure, she had a job that was safe; that was more than some people could say. It was *too* safe, though, and filled with time-consuming, repetitive tasks.

As for home, the condo had felt far too big since the death of her one and only love four years ago.

A couple weeks after Jules's passing, she had found an envelope in a desk drawer with her name written on it with that overly dramatic and fancy loop finishing the L in Jules's characteristic hand. The last card. You never think about it being the last one when you read that quick to-do list scrawled on the back of a piece of junk mail—bread, milk, dry cleaning, taxes… You never think about *anything* being the last one—the last time you separate her clothes from yours in neat little piles on the bed after doing the laundry, the last time you reach for those cookies she likes on the grocery store shelf. It was all she could think about the days, the weeks, the months after Jules's death—all of those last times that she hadn't paid close enough attention to.

Her mother was the one who had convinced her to open the envelope finally. It wasn't healthy to carry it around, "like continually scratching off a scab," she'd said. So, Lexy had opened it. It was a birthday card and inside there was a gift certificate to the community art center and a short note that said, "The world needs more beauty and you're just the gal to create it. Happy Birthday, my love."

All those months of carrying the envelope around with her— all those months of imagining what Jules had said—the wisdom she might have imparted, the love she might have set down in pages and pages of carefully crafted words, poetry perhaps, and the whole time there were just those two little sentences.

Still, she'd wanted to honor the gift. So she'd signed up for Handbuilding Like the Ancients, a class that Jules had taken and raved about, thinking that by handling the clay she might discover something she hadn't known about her partner. She'd continued to sign up for ceramics and sculpture classes long after the gift certificate had been spent because it was her birthday present, after all, and there would be no more of them—at least no more from Jules. This was the last one.

Lexy set up her supplies at her usual station by the octagonal kiln and busied herself with the task of readying the piece she had been working on. She carefully peeled off the damp cloth covering and lightly sprayed the gray stoneware clay with water from a spray bottle. Last week, she had completed only a preliminary form of the figure from feet to torso. She had yet to smooth out any definitive curves and edges. Although it was clear that the figure was female, she was still featureless and coarse. Lexy unloaded her palette knife, crimping pliers, ribbon tool and assorted boxwood tools and sponges from her bag and set them at the ready on the side of her sculpting stand.

The instructor welcomed the class, made mention of a few of the students' pieces and briefly discussed technique. The young nude model then took her place on the small makeshift stage positioned in the center of the room. Stage lights illuminated her body as she stretched out on the distressed wooden boxes.

Lexy plugged in her earbuds, keyed up a Tori Amos album and began to work. She liked the smooth, damp feel of the clay on her fingertips, especially stoneware clay, which had less grog than traditional earthenware.

Smoothing out the thigh and muscular calf of the figure, she let her mind drift to the bar, not yesterday's fiasco but to what had happened the previous Friday and standing in the doorway, so close to Anna. One small move forward and she could have captured those lips with her own. Her fingers worked to shape the figure's breasts and rib, her pulse racing at the thought of her mouth on Anna's, the warmth of her ivory skin, the bend of her slender and graceful neck. Soon her mind was conjuring images of Anna's firm breasts, her hips, her thighs opening for her. Lexy felt herself growing flushed and wet in response. Worried for a moment that her thoughts could be read on her face, after a brief struggle she gave herself permission to dwell there, continuing to smooth out the curves and shape of the figure before her.

\* \* \*

On Friday morning, Jennifer pulled into the St. Petersburg/ Clearwater International Airport and parked in the short-term parking lot. Taking a seat on one of the rattan wicker chairs in the living room-sized lobby, she took out the *Oprah* magazine that she had brought with her from home and flipped to an article on exercises one can do at the office.

About fifteen minutes before their scheduled departure time, a woman dressed in shorts and sandals and a light teal vest that reminded Jennifer of Publix supermarket uniforms, called for all the passengers to bring their baggage over to the counter.

Jennifer had been surprised the first time she'd flown this airline by the bathroom-style scale that was used to weigh the passengers' luggage. They charged a dollar per pound over the twenty-pound per person limit. Jennifer had ended up being charged $17, having not carefully read the airline website's information. She'd also evidently missed the part about the airline's practice of weighing the passengers and was horrified when, in front of the whole group, an attendant announced her weight to the woman with the clipboard.

As they passed the boarding agent, each passenger was handed a fan consisting of cardboard glued to what Jennifer thought looked like a tongue depressor. "Sunny Coast Sea Rides" was printed across each of them in a teal lettering that matched the woman's vest. They looked like a child's arts and crafts project. "The air-conditioning will not be on until we reach maximum altitude," the woman explained as she distributed them.

As Jennifer walked with the crowd toward the plane, she noticed two nicely dressed men leading the way. They must be together, she thought, watching as one of the men slipped two fingers into the other man's back pocket. Someone said something from behind Jennifer that caused the two men to turn toward the sound, and she recognized one of them as Arnold Flemming, her publisher.

"Arnold!" she shouted, waving her magazine in his direction.

Arnold did not respond, nor did he even look toward the voice calling his name. Instead, he turned back to the plane.

She pushed her way through the crowd and grabbed his shoulder, causing both men to turn toward her.

"Arnold!" she said again.

Arnold looked paralyzed by fear. The tanned Ken doll that he was with, however, looked more irritated than horrified. "Look, miss, you've got the wrong person," he said.

Jennifer took in Arnold's stunned expression. "Arnold! What's wrong with you?"

"He's not this Arnold guy you're blabbering on about!" the blonde shouted. His breath smelled medicinal and minty. "This woman's obviously crazy, Ari," he mumbled to his partner.

"Ari?" she asked, taking in Arnold's features. His hair wasn't slicked back with gel as it normally was and sunglasses shielded his eyes from view. But it was Arnold, wasn't it? She suddenly wondered if perhaps the Bloody Mary she had prior to leaving for the airport had been a double instead of a single or if she was suffering from heat stroke or something. "Sorry," she stammered. "I must be mistaken."

The two made their way to the plane, leaving Jennifer utterly confused in their wake.

The plane was tiny, a Piper Chieftain ten-seater charter plane. Jennifer's seat was in the midsection on the left side. To make it into her seat unscathed she had to contort her body into a crouching position so as not to hit her head on the ceiling of the plane. She panicked a little when she thought she recognized the smell in the interior as that of contact cement and spied duct tape holding together a rip in the back of the cloth seat in front of her. Warm with nervousness, she fanned herself with the cardboard on the tongue depressor and waited for takeoff.

Jennifer wished she could turn around to look at the two men seated in the back without drawing undue attention to herself. Quickly exhausting the possibilities, she moved on to more interesting topics: her new book and Andy Cole. She had all but forgotten about the men by the time they landed in Key West.

* * *

The drive to Key West had taken Andy just under eight hours on the turnpike. The Blue Parrot Apartment Complex, near the boardwalk, Andy soon learned, predominantly offered vacation rentals, although the superintendent, a Mr. John Creighton, did live in his unit year-round. "With his fiancée," added the front desk clerk, a pretty, thin, African-American woman in a blazer that was far too large for her small frame. A gold nametag pinned to the lapel read "Adalia Johnson." She'd balked at providing the information until Andy had showed her her ID and shield.

"And which unit might that be, Ms. Johnson?" Andy asked.

The woman punched something into the keyboard. "Twelve A." She turned her deep brown eyes on Andy. "Agent Cole, is there some reason to be concerned?"

"Let's hope not," Andy replied.

Although she liked the excitement of following the case better than the desk duty she had been confined to following her partner Seth's death eighteen months earlier, Andy couldn't help but wish she had met Jennifer under different circumstances. It was totally out of character for her to be attracted to a suspect—the prime suspect, no less, in a murder case. But Jennifer just wasn't capable of... At least she didn't think she was. But then, no one's closet was free of skeletons. She just hoped Jennifer's skeletons were metaphorical and not literal.

Andy thought about her as she continued to walk toward 12A, eying the apartment numbers as she went. About how, under different circumstances, they might have actually had a relationship. Might actually do normal relationship things, like watch prime time television together cuddled on the couch.

*Cuddling on the couch? Nice! What the fuck is wrong with me? How can I lose all sense of ethics for some hot chick? I'm an FBI agent, damn it!*

That title still made her chest swell with pride. Her interest in leadership and service had led her to enroll at The Citadel after 9/11, where she earned a bachelor's degree with a dual major in English and Criminal Justice and then a master's in English. When her girlfriend at the time was accepted as a Fulbright Fellow into a prestigious PhD program at UNH,

Andy followed her to New England and enrolled in the police academy there.

As their relationship fell apart, Andy's career took off. She landed a job in the Patrol Division at the Manchester Police Department. And over the course of the next four years, she worked her way up from community policing to investigations, where she partnered with Seth. Her life had finally settled into an easy rhythm—she had a great job and a new girlfriend, to boot. And then everything came to a screeching halt.

Seth was killed during the pursuit of a teenager suspected of burglary. After the shooting, Andy was assigned to desk duty, a fate that for her was worse than death. Much of the pain and frustration at work leeched into her personal life— so much so that she wasn't surprised to come home to find a farewell letter fixed to the refrigerator and the closet emptied of Kirsten's clothes. Work was just as much of a struggle. She quickly learned that the only way she was ever going to get back in the field was to hide her emotions. It took six months, but eventually her hands stopped shaking every morning as she buttoned up her uniform and she managed to fend off the tears that threatened each time she wrote reports on bookings that had even minor details in common with Seth's shooting. And she learned to smile and joke while all the time railing inside.

Deciding that she needed a change of scenery, maybe even a new job—the familiarity was too much—Andy applied to the FBI and was accepted. She spent twenty weeks at the FBI Academy in Quantico, Virginia. She met Patrick there. The ink on her diploma was barely dry when she received the call inviting her to join the Orlando task force investigating what they'd dubbed the "J. Deveaux Copycat Murders." Even though she was clearly inexperienced, Andy was an obvious choice, given her sexual orientation, her ties to New England and her teaching credentials. While she'd like to imagine that she was selected for her service record and investigative skills, she was also probably one of the only trained agents with the requisite eighteen graduate credits in English to be credentialed to teach at the college level. But that was okay with her. She might be a rookie, but she was a capable rookie with good instincts.

Those instincts told her that Jennifer didn't have anything to do with the murders, but her training reminded her to be careful. This was an important case. And if she screwed this up, it wouldn't be just her career on the line. Lives were at stake.

* * *

Lexy, needing a break from papers, Jennifer and especially thoughts of Anna, skipped her morning workout at the gym on Saturday to sculpt. The studio at the Community Center was empty except for an older woman who was working at a pottery wheel in the far corner of the room. The room felt more peaceful than usual to Lexy with the stage lights extinguished. The white-haired woman acknowledged Lexy's presence with a quick nod of her head and turned her attention back to the wet red clay spinning between her palms.

Lexy emptied her art bag and uncovered her sculpture. The figure lay in the position of the model, on her back with one leg extended and the other propped up at the knee. Her elbows supported the weight of her torso, and her head was tilted slightly back, causing her long hair to fall to the floor and spread out from the point of impact like a waterfall. The model's hair was thin and straight, but Lexy's figure had thick wavy locks, which she envisioned as soft and dark although the model's hair was blond. The clay figure also had smaller but firmer breasts and was thinner and more toned than the size twelve model. There was a hint of rib showing through her skin and her thighs were more muscular than meaty.

Lexy cycled through the musical choices on her iPod, decided on some Beth Orton and plugged in her earbuds. Listening to the sensual, pulsing music, she began to shape the delicate facial features of her figure, starting, as she always did, with the cheekbones and jaw.

To her surprise she found that what emerged as she manipulated the clay was Anna's face, which, since that first meeting at the vending machine, had roved through Lexy's waking and sleeping landscapes as an uninvited guest.

\* \* \*

"Lex, I'm so glad I caught you!" Rand's voice thundered through the earpiece of Lexy's Motorola as she crammed the last bag of groceries into the trunk of her VW Beetle. She crinkled her nose in response and lowered the volume.

"What's up, Rand?" She knew it was another favor. His voice always grew impossibly loud when he was going to ask her for something—as if she was less likely to decline the request the higher the decibel he used to voice it.

"Ari will *kill me* if I don't make it to pick up his dry cleaning before they close for the weekend, and I'm at a nail appointment that's running late. Could you be a doll? Please? Please? Please?"

Lexy sighed. "Okay. The one on Central?"

"That's the one. Oh, you're a lifesaver! I owe you one."

Over the six years that Rand had been her neighbor, he had racked up quite a list of "owed ones." Lexy was curious when exactly he planned to repay her. She had thought that having two men as neighbors would be very helpful when it came to things like lifting heavy furniture, installing a fan or borrowing a screwdriver. But Rand and Ari could help with none of those things. In fact, it was Lexy who lent them her tools, helped Rand move the bureau to the other side of the bedroom and changed the batteries in their smoke detectors. She learned to rely on Rand and Ari for only the things that they were good at: recipes, fashion and gossip.

The dry cleaner's wasn't far from the grocery store. A brief stop there wasn't likely to imperil the well-being of the Häagen-Dazs coffee ice cream she'd just stowed in the trunk. She had actually gone to the frozen food aisle to pick up a much less fattening sorbet. When she saw the Häagen-Dazs shelf, she couldn't resist. Before she could regain control, her cart was twelve hundred calories richer.

At the dry cleaner's the goateed teenager running the register gave her a hard time because she didn't have a claim ticket, but she was finally able to win him over with kindness. She threatened to file a complaint with the Better Business Bureau.

"What was the name?" he said irritably as he watched the merry-go-round of plastic-wrapped clothes on hangers.

"Flemming. Ari Flemming."

The clothes circled endlessly until he hit the button on the wall with his palm. He checked the tag and handed her two blazers wrapped in see-through pink plastic wrap.

* * *

Andy Cole was not prepared for what she found in Apartment 12A at the Blue Parrot Apartment Complex.

When she was able to regain control of her breathing, she leaned against the stucco wall outside Creighton's apartment and punched in the familiar number on her cell.

"Reilly," a voice answered.

"It's Cole. I found Samantha Jensen."

"Yeah? What did you find out?"

"She didn't have much to say, given that she's decapitated and dismembered."

# CHAPTER SIX

Feeling bad about how she had left things with Jennifer, Lexy tried her cell twice on Sunday and again early Monday, Labor Day, but she got her voice mail each time. This concerned her. Jennifer usually answered on the first or second ring and rarely let anyone—aside, of course, from one-night stands she was desperately trying to avoid—go to voice mail. Her new iPhone might as well have been an appendage. It went everywhere she went.

The three-day weekend had allowed Lexy to get caught up on both her grading and her chores around the condo, something that rarely ever happened. While emptying the pockets of her jeans Monday morning to prepare them for the washer, she had come across Eden's card with the sudsy sheepdog on it and remembered her invitation to the barbecue. She wondered if Jennifer might be there.

On a whim she drove to Lexington Avenue, looking for Jennifer's Beamer. It was easy to locate Eden's house—the circular driveway and the street out front were lined with cars.

Not finding Jennifer's BMW among them, she decided to go home. While circling back, though, she unintentionally made eye contact with Charlie, who stopped lifting a case of Budweiser out of the back of her blue van to shout to the person in the passenger seat, "Hey, Rach, Jennifer's friend Lexy's here!"

Lexy waved and slowed the car, but couldn't think of an excuse for leaving before Rachel appeared, tapping on her driver's side window and motioning for her to roll it down. It struck Lexy as odd that people still made that circular rolling motion when most cars came equipped with power windows these days.

"You can park on the grass if there isn't any street parking left," she said. She looked extremely casual in a backward baseball cap, a Women's Music Festival T-shirt that she swam in, obviously Charlie's originally, cargo shorts and flip-flops.

Lexy pulled her car onto the lawn as directed. Her hopes of ducking out of the party early were dashed when she spied a white Ford F-150 in her rearview mirror that seemed likely to park her in.

"So where's the professor?" Charlie asked as she held the gate door open for Lexy.

"Jennifer's not here?"

"We haven't seen her," Rachel answered. "Not even at the bars this weekend."

"It's gotta be some hot, sex-filled escapade." Charlie laughed, elbowing Rachel in the ribs. "We'll hear about it later."

Lexy hoped that she was right, as long as the "escapade" didn't involve Anna, that is.

A flagstone patio surrounded a pretty, lagoon-style pool. Mature elephant ear plants, bougainvilleas and assorted grasses complemented boulder landscape rocks along the circumference of the patio, which was shaded by a few magnolia trees and queen palms. Music was being piped through disguised rock speakers within the boulders, and accent lighting shone upon the plants, adding a more lively flare to the late-afternoon calm.

On the eastern side of the patio, a tiki bar was surrounded by women holding fruity drinks. Lexy breathed a sigh of relief to see so many casually dressed women. Having not planned to attend the party herself, she was wearing the comfortable army green, flat-front men's shorts that she wore when lounging around the house, a button-down shirt and leather sandals. She'd tied her hair back loosely with a brown leather wrap for comfort.

The backyard was filled with women, some of whom Lexy recognized from the bar. Some filled the patio furniture while others lounged in deck chairs or stood in small groups near the bar, the gazebo or the stainless steel grill. Lexy spotted an apron-clad Eden there, waving a spatula in the air as if it were a medieval weapon as she chatted with a butch in men's Bermuda shorts.

Lexy followed Charlie and Rachel to the tiki bar, where a woman dressed in a colorful Guatemalan skirt and matching blouse was serving drinks. Charlie made introductions. "Lexy, this is Paige, Eden's partner. Paige...Lexy."

Instead of a handshake, Paige reached over the bar and enclosed Lexy in a warm hug, managing, in the process, to dip her beaded necklace in a drink she had just finished mixing. Lexy decided at that point to stick to bottled beer.

"Charlie, you better get over there. They'll start the game without you," Paige said, pointing to a glass-topped patio table with a teak umbrella. Charlie scooped two bottled beers out of the ice chest and she and Rachel headed in the direction Paige had pointed. Lexy followed, thinking it best to stick with the people she knew.

* * *

Anna sat on the edge of the pool, dangling her feet in its cool water and reveling in the day's last hour of sunlight. She sipped the pineapple-flavored vodka drink Paige had made for her, almost choking when she saw Lexy Strayer take a seat at the poker table. Her first instinct was to run, but as her eyes fell on the toned legs stretching below the knee-length shorts she wore, a different impulse took shape within her. She gulped

down the rest of her pineapple concoction and went in search
of something stronger. She found it in the kitchen, where she
knocked back two shots of straight vodka.

* * *

"What's the buy-in?" Charlie asked.

"Ten bucks."

Charlie threw a twenty on the table. "This is for me and
Rach." She turned to Lexy, who was sitting behind her. "You
can't play from back there. Scoot up."

"Oh, I'm not playing." Lexy wasn't a card player. In fact, the
last time she handled a deck was when she was six and playing
Crazy Eights with her father. The cards had been decorated
with images of Peanuts characters.

"Come on," coaxed a woman with an unlit cigar between her
teeth. "It'll be fun. We're not *serious* players." Charlie cleared
her throat. "Well, aside from Chuck, that is. Really, we're just
here to have fun."

"All right." Lexy pulled her chair forward and dug in her
pocket for her money. "But you'll have to fill me in on the rules
as we go."

* * *

Anna, still feeling the burn from the shots, headed to the
card table.

"You didn't start yet, did you?" she asked, deliberately
standing behind her professor's chair, so close that she could
smell her perfume. She breathed in deeply, liking the pleasing,
fragrant scent.

Lexy shifted in her chair, perhaps recognizing Anna's voice,
but she didn't turn around to look at her.

"Have a seat. The more players, the larger the pot," the
woman with the now-lit cigar said, waving her in.

Anna sat next to Charlie, two seats to the right of Lexy. As
soon as she got settled and added her money to the pile, she

turned her eyes in Lexy's direction, but the woman was busy making equal stacks of blue chips.

Each player anted, adding one colored chip to the center pile. The dealer, a lanky woman with bronzed skin, announced, "Seven card stud with twos wild." She dealt while intermittently fanning the air with her hand. "Cheryl, why do you insist on smoking those things every time we play?"

"It's tradition!"

"And *stud* means what exactly?" Anna whispered in Charlie's ear.

"Besides me?" Charlie laughed as she meticulously arranged her poker hand. "It means you've got what you got. No picking up."

Anna stole glances to her left every so often, but Lexy seemed determined not to notice her.

"What's wild again? Fours?" Rachel asked.

"Twos!" three of the women shouted in unison.

Rachel started the betting with two chips. Lexy folded early, having only a pair of threes and no wild cards. Charlie raised five chips, which caused three other women to bow out, including Rachel and Anna.

Anna took off the open blouse she wore over her bathing suit top, hoping that would encourage Lexy to notice her. She threw the shirt over the back of her chair and stretched by lifting her arms and arching her back. The butch seated across from her certainly noticed, running her eyes over Anna's neck and shoulders appreciatively, but not Lexy.

Charlie won the first hand.

Rachel shuffled, it being her turn to deal, and announced the second game, "Queens and What Follows."

By the eighth game, it had grown dark. Having lost almost all of her chips and feeling frustrated with Lexy's refusal to even look at her, Anna pointed to the cigar Cheryl was smoking and asked, "You got any more of those?"

"Sure," she said, handing Anna one from the pack.

Before Cheryl had a chance to pass the lighter to her, Anna placed the cigar between her lips and stood, stretching her torso over the table toward the woman as seductively as she could manage. A smiling Cheryl lit the end of the cigar as Anna puffed twice with her eyes closed.

\* \* \*

Lexy couldn't help but see the scene unfolding before her. Anna's body was splayed out within arm's reach, her breasts in plain sight and the bare flesh of her stomach, her shoulders, her arms exposed. Lexy's mouth watered in response. She couldn't tear her eyes away. As Anna returned slowly to her chair, she turned her deep green eyes on Lexy, holding her hostage until the spell was broken by Charlie, asking, "Well? What do ya got, Lexy?"

Lexy got her bearings, embarrassed that she had been ogling the younger woman, and fanned her cards out in front of her. "A straight."

"Good, but not good enough." Charlie dropped her cards on the table face up and pulled the huge pot of chips toward her with both hands. "Royal flush."

"Well, that wipes me out." Lexy drained her third beer of the night and stole a quick nervous glance at Anna.

Anna's eyes hadn't left Lexy. "You know, I think I'm throwing in the towel too," she said, snubbing out the cigar that she had barely smoked.

"Well, I enjoyed taking your money." Charlie laughed.

"It's not over yet." Rachel pinched her partner's arm, which produced a yelp from the tall woman. Charlie rubbed at the spot and pouted like a hurt puppy.

To Lexy's dismay, Anna followed her toward a couple of empty deck chairs.

\* \* \*

"So, is it still okay if I call you Lexy?" Anna asked as they seated themselves.

"Sure. We're not at school." Lexy sat down, hugging her knees into her chest with her arm.

"You uncomfortable?" Anna asked.

"What? No, why?"

"Well, look at the guarded way you're sitting."

Lexy repositioned herself so that her legs were stretched out in front of her, crossing them at the ankles. "Maybe a little," she confessed.

"Can you pretend I'm not your student—just for now?"

"Easier said than done."

"I wanted to talk to you about the other night at the bar." Anna turned to face Lexy, whose attention seemed to be focused on the flickering flames of a distant fire pit. "With Jennifer," she added.

"You don't owe me any kind of explanation." The words tumbled out of Lexy as if they had been rehearsed. "You're certainly allowed to do whatever you want, and I'm your teacher, so your personal life has nothing—"

"Listen, I'm really not interested in your friend." Anna stared at the side of Lexy's face, trying to gauge her reaction. "Not at all," she added for emphasis.

"That has nothing to do with me."

There was a long pause before Anna spoke again. "Do you know anything about the stars?"

\* \* \*

"The stars? Not much." Anna's question took Lexy back to her adolescence and the glow-in-the-dark stars on the ceiling of her childhood bedroom. She hadn't even opened the package completely before she started to stick them on. She had placed them about a half an inch apart until she realized that if she continued in that pattern she would quickly run out of stars and have only one big glob of neon oddly placed in the right corner of her bedroom. By then, though, it was too late. The tiny galaxy became a source of comfort in time, rather than a cause for self-criticism, a calming presence as she fell asleep or when, furious with her parents, she retreated to her bedroom and lay there staring up at it. The stars hadn't held the same soothing significance for her father, who had a hell of a time scraping them off before they sold the house.

"That's Andromeda there." Lexy's eyes followed Anna's outstretched arm to a grouping of stars that looked a bit like a stick figure. "Do you see?" she asked. "One of her arms seems to be attached to something long, like a sword? She looks like a warrior."

"Queen of Mycenae."

"What?"

"Andromeda, in Greek mythology, she was a princess rescued by Perseus. She later married him and became queen. Her name derives from the Latin. It means 'to think of a man.'"

"A *man*?" Anna laughed. "I guess I should use another constellation to impress women then."

Lexy smiled. "So I've walked into some sort of trap, have I?"

"That's right. First, I impress you with my knowledge of the constellations and then I recite some sonnets...I thought I'd skip the sonnets, though, you being a literature professor and all." Lexy laughed. Feeling much more at ease with Anna, she chatted comfortably with her until Eden requested Anna's "bartender expertise" to concoct a specialty drink at the tiki bar.

Lexy took the opportunity to investigate the rest of the large open yard, admiring the boulder landscaping as she walked along the perimeter. Coming to a small cedar gazebo, she peered into its dimly lit interior. Inside she saw a short-haired woman holding another woman in her arms from behind, kissing her neck and ear as her fingers plucked at the buttons of her blouse. The couple was oblivious to Lexy's presence, and although she knew she should leave, she was drawn to the intimate scene.

The short-haired woman slipped her hand inside her companion's now open shirt and massaged her breasts, pulling at her nipples with her fingers and eliciting a slight moan from her lips. As a hand slid to the button on the woman's jeans and slowly peeled down its zipper, Lexy felt her own heartbeat quickening. The hand disappeared in her partner's jeans while the other continued to massage her breast and the woman's breathing became shallower, faster. Lexy's did too. A warmth rushed through her, settling between her legs, her body responding as if she were the one being touched.

Intent on the scene in front of her, Lexy was startled to feel hot breath on her ear and hear the whisper of a sexy voice. "What are you doing out here...*Professor?*"

Turning around, Lexy found Anna facing her, the light from the fire intermittently revealing her bare midriff. Without thinking, she reached for Anna, placing a hand on her wonderfully flat stomach.

* * *

Anna felt her body instantly come alive, the touch electrifying her skin. She heard Lexy's ragged breathing, saw her eyes grow even darker, and she knew what she wanted. She slowly pulled the leather wrap from Lexy's hair and watched as her honey-brown locks cascaded over her shoulders. She was reaching up to run her fingers through them when Lexy suddenly pulled away, her hand leaving Anna's body and moving to her own parted lips in alarm.

"This can't happen," she said in a shaky voice, taking a step back.

The place on her stomach where Lexy's hand had been felt cold, and Anna shivered.

The younger woman's lips shaped the word "Please" although no sound accompanied the movement. Anna feared that if Lexy didn't touch her again, she might cry.

Lexy, breaking the connection, abruptly turned and walked away from her, back to the party, but not before Anna saw the conflicting emotions playing over her face. She didn't want to leave, Anna thought, or at least part of her didn't.

# CHAPTER SEVEN

Anna sat in the laundromat on Wednesday afternoon watching some soap opera on the television with the rabbit ears that got terrible reception. A handsome, strong-jawed man wearing a white lab coat was flailing his arms in front of a pretty blonde whose lips were painted geisha red. Although the television was muted, Anna assumed that he was a surgeon and arguing with his lover about which one of them was responsible for killing his patient. She had decided, watching their lips move, that it was a Spanish show, since she thought she saw someone mouth the words *"Hola. ¿Cómo estás?"* the only Spanish phrase she knew.

Anna didn't really care about the show. She was just staring, glassy-eyed, at the fuzzy static dots ripping through the screen like lightning because she didn't like to leave her laundry in the machines without being present for fear that someone would steal her towels or rifle through her underwear.

Glancing at the round plastic clock on the wood-paneled wall to her right, she realized that ordinarily she would be in Lexy's classroom right now. She sipped her Diet Pepsi and watched as her whites tumbled around in the dryer window. *Coward*, she thought angrily, feeling tears threatening to come once more.

\* \* \*

Lexy was relieved to see Anna's chair empty on the Wednesday after the Labor Day party because she had no idea how she was going to endure an hour and fifteen minutes of teaching with Anna's eyes on her. She found the prospect that Anna might want to discuss what had happened even more terrifying.

Lexy was also relieved that Jennifer had finally resurfaced on Wednesday, having secured a substitute for her Tuesday classes. Although Jennifer avoided answering questions about her weekend, she seemed refreshed and didn't appear to be harboring any ill feelings toward Lexy about their phone conversation on Thursday. In fact, it was business as usual as they sipped their coffees in the cafeteria on Wednesday afternoon.

Jennifer was flipping through the *Orange County Gazette*, the local newspaper, looking for clothing sales while Lexy was mindlessly marking grammatical errors in a freshman composition.

"Remember that student I mentioned a while ago?" Lexy asked.

"The plagiarist?"

"No, not that one." She pushed the stack of blue books aside.

"Brown-nosing Brian?"

"No, the one I said I was attracted to," she whispered.

"Right, yeah, what about her?" Jennifer continued flipping newspaper pages.

"Well, there have sort of been developments."

"You dog!" Jennifer threw her balled-up straw wrapper at Lexy. It landed in her lap.

"Look, I'm really having a problem here," she whispered, brushing the wrapper onto the floor. "Can you be serious for once?"

Jennifer closed the newspaper and looked at Lexy with concern. "Do tell."

"I made a mistake." Lexy blushed, thinking of the gazebo. "I almost...I mean, I touched her."

Jennifer looked completely shocked. "Oh my god! Just give me a second to pick my chin up off the floor. What do you mean you *touched* her?"

"It's hard to explain." Lexy pinched the bridge of her nose, trying to stop the headache that was beginning to form. "She was at that Labor Day party at Eden's and we flirted a little. I was drinking. I stopped myself before anything actually happened, but I did put my hand on her abdomen."

"Lexy, I'm so surprised. I didn't know you had it in you—almost molesting a teenager!"

Embarrassed, Lexy said in a quiet but stern voice, "Will you keep your voice down? And she's not a teenager. She's in her late twenties."

"So why did you stop?"

Lexy was growing angrier by the second. "You know, if you're going to make light of this—"

"Hold on," Jennifer said, grabbing hold of Lexy's hand. "I'm sorry. Look, nothing happened. You have nothing to worry about."

"What if she complains to the dean?"

"Why would she when she wants to get you in the sack? Besides, you're tenured. What the hell are you worried about?"

"Remember Whitaker?" Richard Whitaker, a tenured instructor at OCC, had been terminated after a year-long criminal investigation proved that he had sexually harassed a female student.

"Are you sending her pictures of parts of your anatomy?" Whitaker had used one of the college's fax machines to send the student a photograph of his privates.

Horrified, Lexy hissed, "Of course not!"

"Then it isn't the same situation."

Jennifer reopened the newspaper to a random page. Lexy's eyes fell on a couple of headlines: "NOAA Predicts Above-

Normal Atlantic Hurricane Season..." "Local Woman Found Decapitated in Key West Apartment..."

"You're grown adults, Lex. It's frowned on, but there's no actual pol—" She stopped mid-word. "Holy shit!" The outburst caused students at the neighboring tables to drop their silverware and turn toward Jennifer and Lexy.

"What is it?"

"Half off at Nordstrom!"

\* \* \*

"B-But," the eighteen-year-old girl in Jennifer's office blubbered, smearing her mascara with a balled-up tissue, "I've never gotten anything less than a B."

"I understand, but college is more demanding than high school." Jennifer wished the girl would leave her office so that she could get back to her Internet surfing. She had been in the process of searching for shoes to match the Liz Claiborne outfit she had picked up at the mall the previous weekend.

Tears dripped onto the girl's orange notebook cover, leaving darkened spots.

"Look, Cecelia, the class isn't over yet. You still have the research paper, which is worth fifteen percent of your grade. So it's not impossible for you to finish with a B. You just have to apply yourself."

The girl sniffled. Jennifer wondered if that was a good sign.

A husky voice interrupted her thoughts: "Knock, knock." Andy Cole's dark head of hair appeared in the doorframe.

"Hey!" Jennifer said cheerily, though she was still seething about Andy's brush-off the previous Thursday. Turning her attention back to the blubbering girl, she said, "Cecelia, Professor Cole and I need to discuss something very important, so if you wouldn't mind..."

The girl slowly and methodically pushed her tear-stained notebook into her bag.

After the girl exited, Jennifer turned searching eyes on Andy. "So, am I to assume that your...*busyness* has dissipated enough to allow some time for polite conversation?"

Andy frowned. "Sorry I was so short. I…well, it was a bad day."

"And today is better?"

"It's looking up." Andy raised two motorcycle helmets, one in each hand, and asked, "How about that ride, Professor Gardiner?"

Jennifer almost bounced out of her seat. "Let's go!"

The midsized motorcycle in the faculty parking lot had brooding and sexy lines, Jennifer thought. Its chrome reflected the light brilliantly, and she especially liked the flare of mulberry red on the body casing of the handsome masculine bike. Andy swung her leg over the black gunslinger seat effortlessly and motioned for Jennifer to join her.

Jennifer climbed onto the seat, positioning herself behind the other woman's tall, broad frame.

The bike came to life. Jennifer liked the way the engine rumbled between her legs. She slid closer to Andy, pressing her breasts against the woman's back and wrapping her arms around her stomach. She felt the hard abdominal muscles under her fingers and couldn't help but become turned on.

"You okay?" Andy shouted through the whipping wind as they drove.

"Oh yeah." She could feel herself grow wet and swollen from the movement between her legs and the strong woman that she was clinging to. She allowed one of her hands to travel from Andy's abdomen to her upper thigh, half expecting to be stopped. But she wasn't.

* * *

Andy didn't know what to do—her mind was racing. It had been so long since she'd been intimate with anyone that she grew incredibly excited by just the contact of their bodies. As Jennifer's hand began to travel downward, she knew she should stop her. Jennifer was the prime suspect in a murder investigation, for Christ's sake. There wasn't much that she could do that would be more unethical than this—except maybe planting evidence or coercing a confession. If anyone found out, she'd be done—she'd lose not only her job but also the respect of her colleagues—and she should. It was wrong, *really* wrong. But she didn't want to stop. It felt too good.

When Jennifer undid the clasp and zipper of Andy's pants and slowly slid her hand inside, Andy lifted her body slightly in response, providing Jennifer with the room she needed to cup Andy's warm center in her palm.

Andy had lost herself completely in the feeling of the woman's hands on her—claiming her. She felt fingers brush over her swollen clit. Once. Twice. Then moving in languid circles. She felt herself grow hard and fought the instinct to shut her eyes.

When Jennifer slipped two fingers inside her, Andy's body responded by grinding her hips into the seat. She wanted to be filled.

She was going to come. Afraid that she might lose control of the bike when she did, she stilled Jennifer's hand by gripping her wrist. "Wait!" she said.

Andy was surprised—and excited—by how quickly Jennifer was able to pin her to the wall in the foyer after they entered her house. Holding Andy's wrists with one hand, she unbuttoned her shirt deftly with the other.

When Jennifer's fingers closed around a hard nipple, Andy's eyelids fluttered shut. "I want you so bad," she breathed.

Jennifer dropped to her knees and began sliding Andy's pants down over her muscular thighs. Their eyes met for just a moment, and Andy saw a hunger in those blue oceans that made her even wetter.

"Kiss me...please?" Andy said, her pleading voice sounding foreign to her own ears.

Jennifer pulled herself erect. She grabbed a fistful of Andy's hair, forcefully pulling her head back, and said, "Beg me."

With that, Andy was flooded with desire. "Please?" she begged. "Please?"

"Good girl." Jennifer ran her tongue along Andy's bottom lip. She opened her mouth, inviting her in. The kiss was sensual at first and grew forceful, as Andy felt Jennifer's hands claim her breasts once again.

Andy *needed* to touch her. She'd never needed anything more desperately than she needed to feel this woman's body. She reached for her, but only felt warm flesh for a moment because her hand was captured. "Did I say you could touch?" Jennifer asked coldly.

"Please?" she said, reaching again.

She was surprised when she felt the stinging smack on her cheek. "You touch when I say touch!"

"Yes," Andy complied, growing impossibly turned on by the thought of being dominated.

She was led to the bedroom, where Jennifer finished undressing her. Before she knew what was happening, her hands were tied together with a leather belt, her feet were strapped to the bedposts so that her legs were spread wide apart and her eyes were covered by a blindfold.

She strained to feel with her skin but felt nothing except for the air when she moved. It was quiet for a long time, too long, and Andy began to panic. *My god, what am I doing? I've let a suspect tie me up!* She struggled to wriggle her hands free, but the tie that held them was strong and tight. The sudden feeling of warm flesh against her thigh made her forget her interest in freeing herself. Breasts. Jennifer's breasts. She could feel the supple fullness and the hard nipples passing over her lower abdomen now. And she heard a low moan, almost a growl. "You're so sexy," the sultry voice said, as its owner explored her curves with her hands. "I want to taste you."

Andy felt warm breath pass over her swollen clit and she gasped. Jennifer kissed her there and then explored the silky folds of Andy's center with her tongue. She was quickly climbing again toward climax. She couldn't help but moan out loud. "I'm going to come," she managed to say through her ragged breathing.

Jennifer's mouth suddenly disappeared, leaving her cold. "Not yet," she heard her say.

Jennifer untied Andy's hands and guided one to where *she* obviously wanted to be touched, pushing her hard into her wetness. Andy massaged the impossibly wet silky folds with her fingers. "You feel so good," she murmured.

She heard Jennifer's breathing grow ragged. "Yes," she moaned, as she began grinding her hips into Andy's hand. "Fuck me!" she commanded, her hand returning to Andy's clit.

Andy slipped two fingers inside.

"Oh, yes! God, yes! Don't stop!" Jennifer was rocking violently on Andy's fingers now, chanting, "Deeper! Don't stop!"

Andy didn't stop. She felt the pressure on her clit grow harder and the movements more insistent as Jennifer's muscles closed tightly around her fingers.

"Yes!" Jennifer was shouting at the top of her lungs. "Andy! Yes! Yes!"

Andy couldn't stop herself from climaxing when she heard Jennifer scream her name and felt the muscles encasing her fingers spasm violently.

She grabbed at the blindfold, desperate to see, but Jennifer stopped her. "I'm not done yet," she growled.

* * *

They had sex for hours. In the early morning, before the sun came up, Jennifer stared at the sleeping woman in her bed. It was rare that she allowed anyone to stay overnight; in fact, the last woman to share her bed was Samantha—that lying cheat. She'd let Samantha and her beagle Max move in with her, even put her name on the lease—it was easier than keeping a drawer of toiletries and a change of clothes at each other's places and, to be honest, she liked having easy access to her. Samantha wasn't clingy and was good in bed, so it seemed the ideal arrangement. She could still remember the way that Samantha would innocently grab the dog's leash off the counter, whistle for Max, and announce, "We're going for a walk." It wasn't until she'd opened Samantha's cell phone bill, mistaking it for her own, that Jennifer realized the real reason for the all-too-frequent walks. She was calling *him*—the him with the Christian Slater voice who answered when Jennifer dialed the number listed on the bill seventy-two times. The him who lived just four blocks away.

Andy wasn't like that, Jennifer thought as she watched the slow rise and fall of the woman's chest. For one thing, she was a lot smarter than Samantha, perhaps even as smart as Jennifer herself, which was something she had found enticing about her. Andy was solid, physically and otherwise, and dependable, even predictable. Jennifer liked that about her.

* * *

Andy's eyes fluttered open. Seeing Jennifer beside her brought a rush of desire combined with self-loathing. *How could I?* The blue eyes that held hers smiled. As she looked into the woman's angelic face, her lips swollen from kissing and her chameleon eyes suddenly growing lighter like the sky, Andy thought that it wasn't hard to imagine that someone could be so obsessed with Jennifer that she'd want to eliminate anyone who'd hurt her.

"You know, when I stopped by your office last Thursday, you seemed different somehow. I thought you weren't interested in me." Jennifer smiled coyly.

"Clearly, you were mistaken."

"Were you visiting a girlfriend last weekend?"

The genuine concern in Jennifer's face almost caused Andy to tell her the truth. "Visiting a friend in Key West."

"*Just* a friend?" Jennifer played with Andy's hair.

"Yes, just a friend."

# CHAPTER EIGHT

It was late. The digital clock on her nightstand read 3:43 a.m. Lexy had been awakened by loud voices in the condo next door. She couldn't make out the words, but she could distinguish Rand's high-pitched Dom DeLuise whine from Ari's more masculine tone. She heard something hit the wall; her bedroom wall abutted their living room. Ari had had a carpenter install shelving on the wall, shelves that held pictures of Princess in various outfits and Rand and Ari posing in front of the Eiffel Tower, Mayan ruins and the Stonewall Bar in the Village.

Lexy sat up in bed and put her ear to the wall. For a few minutes, she heard nothing, and then there was the distinctive slamming of the front door.

She jumped when the phone rang.

"Hello?" She could only make out sobbing. "Rand?"

"He's having an affair."

"I'm coming over." Lexy pulled on her pajama top— she was already wearing the bottoms—and her slippers. She rummaged through the kitchen cupboard, grabbing a bag of mini marshmallows and a box of instant cocoa and trotted next door.

When Rand opened the door, his eyes, normally vibrant and youthful, were puffy and red. "Oh, sweetie, I'm so sorry." She wrapped her arms around his doughboy abs.

"Nice penguins," Rand said, commenting on the print of her flannel pajamas. The pajamas, left over from Lexy's time living in Maine, featured penguins wearing little red scarves and winter hats. They were far too warm for even her air-conditioned condo, but Lexy still wore them because they reminded her of her time with Jules.

Rand waited on the couch with a box of tissues, dabbing periodically at his eyes, as she made the cocoa.

"I don't understand," he was saying. "Six years, Lex! How *could* he?"

"Did he confess or did you catch him in the act?" She set the kettle on the burner and poured the contents of two Swiss Miss packets into ceramic mugs she'd found in one of the kitchen cabinets.

"There was a receipt from a restaurant in Key West in his pants pocket. I found it while doing the laundry." Rand sobbed a little before continuing. "It was from Labor Day weekend. He had told me..." Tears gushed at this point. "He-He was meeting with a business client in Clearwater!" Princess, who had been doing a confused dance on the couch cushion, stopped and looked at Rand, turning her head to the side as if in question.

Lexy, waiting for the water to boil, joined Rand in the living room. She smoothed his bleached blond hair back with her fingers. "And then you confronted him?" He nodded solemnly. "And he confessed?"

His hands rubbed at his eyes; he looked suddenly very childlike. "He met the guy in a chat room. He claims it was a one-time thing."

"But you don't believe him," Lexy said matter-of-factly as she rubbed small circles between his shoulder blades.

"No. He *lied* to me!" Princess nudged at Rand's hand with her nose in concern.

The kettle whistled, and Lexy gave Rand's neck a quick squeeze before heading to the kitchen again.

"Oh, Lexy, what am I going to do?" he whined as she plopped a small handful of marshmallows into each steaming mug.

"You're going to do what any respectable queen does when this happens," she said, setting the mugs down on the marble coffee table. "You're going to get out your Bette Davis and Katharine Hepburn movies, and we're going to stay up all night, cry ourselves out and drink cocoa. I'll even let you paint my nails, if you want."

He smiled for the first time since she'd arrived. "Thanks," he said, picking up the steaming mug from the table. Eyeing Lexy's nails, he added, "I'm thinking a nice eggplant frost."

\* \* \*

"Cole here," Andy answered her cell.

"I just faxed you the coroner's packet on the Jensen girl from Key West," Reilly said. Andy could hear the rustling of crinkly paper and imagined her partner was unwrapping his fast-food breakfast—clearly opting to not follow his wife's request that he eat Cheerios or oatmeal to keep his cholesterol in check.

"Cause of death?"

"Multiple stab wounds to the neck and trunk, causing massive hemorrhage."

"What do we know about the perp?"

"Right-handed assailant. The stabbing was calculated and unemotional." Andy fished the papers out of her printer bay and stared at the scanned image of the coroner's photograph of the severed head, marked Case # 69-0130. She felt her own breakfast threaten to resurface. She swallowed.

"The mutilation was postmortem with a hacksaw or similar instrument."

Reading from the papers, she said matter-of-factly, "Time of death, determined by core body temperature, estimated to be three thirty p.m." She searched through the pages for the forensic evidence. "No prints?"

"Clean again," Reilly said. "The only link to the other cases is the victim's sexual orientation and, of course, Deveaux's books." After a beat, he added, "They did find a piece of jewelry that didn't belong to the victim, at least according to the boyfriend, a diamond earring ground into the rug. That could indicate the perp was female...or a guy with expensive tastes. By the way, good call on the snow globe." When investigating the crime scene, Andy had noticed a dust-free circle on a shelf filled with snow globes. Samantha Jensen had had more than two dozen of them, an odd collectible for a Florida native. "There was one missing. The boyfriend couldn't tell us which one, though, or where it might have been from. He's going to see if he can find a photo that might help us identify it."

"Has the boyfriend been cleared? He had a prior domestic, right?"

"Yeah, his kiteboarding alibi was confirmed by a street vendor."

*When the press gets a hold of this, it'll be everywhere, with Jennifer's name attached to it,* Andy thought as she popped two Excedrin onto her tongue.

"Any news on Gardiner?"

Andy grimaced when the pills started to dissolve. She looked for her water bottle. "Jennifer Gardiner might be a lot of things, but she's no killer, Patrick." Finding the blue sport bottle and taking a sip, she added, "Call it instinct."

"So what now?"

"Might be an obsessed fan. If so, she or he would've probably reached out to Gardiner—tried to make contact with her somehow, maybe scared her. I'll do some digging."

\* \* \*

Damn. She was doing it again, Lexy realized. This was the second time she'd found herself driving past Hannah B's on her route home from the Community Center. Doing so took eight more minutes than her usual route, but somehow it was comforting to know that Anna was inside the small shingled building even though she never actually saw her in the parking lot or through the sometimes open door.

This particular evening, however, Lexy found herself pulling into the gravel parking lot. She sat in the idling car and contemplated going inside. Anna had returned to class after missing the one after the Labor Day party but had been quiet and withdrawn since then. Her reader response journals were exemplary as usual, but she rarely smiled or talked in class. Maybe Lexy should apologize or at least offer Anna an explanation.

She decided to go in, have a drink to calm her nerves. Hell, who was she kidding? She wanted to see *her*—if for no reason than the opportunity to look directly into those amazing green eyes. In class she had avoided eye contact, for fear of losing her composure, so although they had spent three hours in the same room together after the Labor Day party, she hadn't really *seen* Anna since then.

It was raining, and Lexy realized she had left her umbrella at the office. *So much for a good hair day.* With that thought, she opened her driver's-side door and made a run for Hannah B's main entrance. Her hair and clothes were dripping by the time she got inside.

Eden, wearing a green and orange tie-dye T-shirt and patched baggy jeans, was working the door again. "My goddess!" she exclaimed. "You're drenched!"

"I'll dry." Lexy smiled, shaking what water she could from her hair. "Good to see you, Eden."

"Nice to see you, Professor." She gestured toward the bar. "Not much of a rocking crowd tonight, I'm afraid." There were only five women at the main bar and a few couples at the tables. The dance floor was empty and only one pool table was occupied.

"That's okay. I just thought I'd have a drink on my way home."

"Well, that we do have."

Lexy made her way to the bar, her eyes searching for Anna. She saw the spiky-haired bartender who had served Jennifer and her on that memorable Friday, but no Anna.

"What'll it be?" the bartender asked.

Lexy glanced at the bottles on the shelf. She wasn't really much of a drinker and she shuddered at the memory of the Jager Bomb that Jennifer had ordered for her. "Do you have red wine?"

"Yeah. We've got Robert Mondavi, Ravenswood..."

"That's fine. A Ravenswood cabernet, please." Her nightly glass of wine had almost become a ritual. She had even started joking with her colleagues about "wining down" after work.

While the bartender filled her glass, Lexy surveyed her surroundings. "Is Anna working tonight?" Almost as soon as the words escaped her lips, she started worrying that the bartender might tell Anna that she had asked about her.

"No, she's off." Lexy, disappointed, wished she had asked before ordering. "That's six dollars." Accepting the ten-dollar bill Lexy pushed her way, she added, "She's over there," nodding in the direction of the pool tables.

Lexy turned around, and she immediately saw her. She was sitting at a booth in the corner. Her head was down. Her thick dark hair hung loosely around her face, and she was writing... no, sketching, Lexy assumed, since her hand was moving in brisk strokes across the pad.

She was alone.

After collecting her change and leaving a tip on the bar, Lexy made her way over to the booth, growing more and more nervous as she neared the young woman.

Anna was too immersed in what she was working on to notice her arrival at first.

"Hi," Lexy said.

Anna's eyes lifted. There was a slight tremor in her bottom lip. "Dr. Strayer? What are you doing here?"

Lexy pointed to her glass. "Just thought I'd stop in for an after-class drink on my way home."

"You teach night classes?" Anna motioned for Lexy to sit down.

"No, I *take* a class—sculpting at the Community Center."

Anna smiled.

"So if you have the night off, why are you still here?"

"I don't feel like going home to my empty apartment yet, I guess."

"What about Ginger?"

"How do you know about Ginger?"

"You mentioned the TV star the first day of class."

"That's right, I did." She kinked an eyebrow. "Do you remember all the students' statements?"

Lexy swallowed nervously. Did she? No, of course she didn't. But she remembered Anna's. That thought made her uncomfortable.

"So, what do you sculpt at this sculpting class you're taking?" Anna asked, perhaps sensing that she didn't want to answer the question.

Lexy blushed, thinking of the nude she was working on. "Women mostly. There's a live model."

"Are you any good?"

"I don't know. I like it though. It's relaxing."

"And sensual, I would bet."

Lexy reddened. "Sometimes."

"Maybe you'd show me your work?"

"Maybe." Lexy sipped her wine, thinking how wonderful it would be if she had met Anna under different circumstances. They could have met at the grocery store when their carts collided, or they could have eyed each other in the waiting room of some doctor's office, or they could have bumped hands reaching for a lemon at the farmers market, or they could have been seated next to each other in a movie theater and struck up a conversation. Of all the possible settings, why did it have to be her classroom?

"What are you thinking about?" Anna asked.

"I was imagining if we had met under different circumstances."

"Yeah, like where?"

"You know, the grocery store or some mundane location."

"Do you think the Andromeda constellation story would have worked better in a grocery store?"

Lexy laughed. Feeling more comfortable, she confessed, "I didn't really come for the drink, Anna."

"No?"

"No, I came here because I wanted to see you. Because I wanted to explain." Anna closed her sketchpad. "I'm sorry that *that* happened at the party. It shouldn't have. *I* shouldn't have."

\* \* \*

Anna took a deep breath, trying to steel her nerves. She would not put her tail between her legs, and she would not let this woman slip away that easily. "I'm not a kid, Lexy. You didn't take advantage of me. And I'm not going to apologize for being attracted to you. In fact, I think you look incredibly sexy right now with your hair wet, and I'm not sorry for thinking that either."

Lexy glanced at the other patrons. "This isn't how I thought this conversation would go," she said.

Anna touched Lexy's hand. "Tell me about how we met in the grocery store."

"Our carts collided." Lexy smiled.

"I hope I didn't hurt you."

"No, it was more of a light tap."

"And then what happened?"

"I didn't get that far yet."

Anna smiled seductively. "I can think of several plotlines."

"I bet." Lexy laughed.

"If I really did hit, I mean 'lightly tap' you with my cart, would you have let me take you out to dinner?"

Lexy paused. "Yes."

"When do you go grocery shopping?"

"Anna, I can't have anything but a professional relationship with you while you're my student."

Anna reached over to catch a drip of rainwater before it fell from Lexy's chin. "Then I'll drop out of your class."

"God, no!" Lexy looked alarmed. "Why should you let the work that you've done already go to waste? I don't want to be the cause of that! And your tuition money!"

Anna sighed. "I want to get to know you, Lexy. I like you."

"Anna, it's unethical for us to be anything but friendly."

Anna considered what friendship with Lexy Strayer would be like. "Friends go out to dinner."

Lexy laughed. "Platonic friends."

"How about tomorrow night...Italian?" Anna smiled. "I'll keep my hands to myself. Promise." She crossed her chest with her fingers.

"How about Vietnamese?" she said. "And lunch instead of dinner?"

Vietnamese in the afternoon would be much less *Lady and the Tramp* romantic than Italian in a candlelit restaurant, Anna thought. Still, it would be a start. "Vietnamese it is." She smiled, feeling elated.

* * *

"Have a seat, Agent." Dr. Rosemary J. Lenar motioned to the leather couch. "How are things?" Andy had been seeing Dr. Lenar regularly at her Lakeland office since moving to Florida. Lenar wasn't the first mental health professional she'd seen, of course. In accordance with the Officer-Involved Shooting Guidelines, she was required to see a police psychologist after her partner Seth had been killed. For six months afterward, Andy had attended weekly meetings with the police shrink. Upon the recommendations of the chief of police, Internal Affairs and the psychologist, she was returned to active duty. The chief, however, encouraged her to continue private counseling, probably sensing that she had not completely recovered. She didn't heed his advice. Not at first anyway. She'd thought, at the time, that she just needed a change of scenery—to get some distance from all the things that reminded her of him. But she found that no amount of distance could trick her brain into forgetting about what had happened—forgetting about *him*. She was more faithful than she wanted to be.

Andy remembered very little of the incident itself, but she could still recall the coppery, organic smell of the blood on her clothes and in her hair. The smell had seemed to linger through multiple launderings and shampoos, plaguing her for weeks after the shooting. To this day, there were still moments when she thought she could smell it.

"I'm fine."

Dr. Lenar opened a manila file folder that had been resting in her lap and readied her expensive-looking fountain pen. "Are you still having blackouts?"

"Occasionally."

"When was the last?"

Andy thought back to waking up bewildered on the beach in Key West. She had been sweaty, her clothes literally soaked through. "I lost an hour over Labor Day weekend."

Dr. Lenar made a note in the folder. "Did anything trigger it this time?"

It happened before she had even gone to the Blue Parrot so it certainly wasn't brought on by the shock of the murder scene. "Not that I know of."

"Were you drinking?"

Andy shook her head emphatically. "I haven't had a drink since Seth's..." Her voice trailed off. She felt her chest constrict.

Dr. Lenar promptly scrawled a note in the folder. "Have you been able to do what we discussed?"

The answer to that would be no. The case file was still sitting on the coffee table in her living room. She had opened it only once. Her whole body had reacted to the photograph clipped to the front of the report—the photograph of Seth's killer, Zachary Taylor, a boy of just seventeen. His expression held no hint of guilt or even awareness of what he had done. It was as if he had been plucked off the street—perhaps right out of a neighborhood game of kickball or something—and placed there without explanation. In his hands was a placard containing his name, date, weight and booking ID.

Upon seeing Zachary's face, Andy hadn't felt the anger she expected to feel; rather, she felt overwhelmed with sadness—a deep and terrifying sadness. So much so that she actually started hyperventilating. She had shut the folder promptly and put her head between her legs in an attempt to regain her composure.

"I couldn't," she said to Dr. Lenar.

"I really think that revisiting the details of the trauma would be therapeutic for you." Andy looked dejectedly at the floor. "Maybe we should try together?"

Andy felt a shiver of fear at the suggestion. "I'd rather do it on my own."

"So you'll try again?"

Andy nodded.

"How about the sleep disturbances?"

"I still have the nightmares." Actually, there was just one and it was always the same. In the dream, Seth was dangling off the side of a building, pleading with Andy not to let go. Andy gripped his fingers in her own and struggled to position her weight so that she could pull him back up onto the roof. And every time she felt her hand open. Oddly, though, it wasn't as if he *slipped* out of her grasp. It was more of a conscious decision, on her part, to let go. The scream that Seth emitted as he fell seemed to reverberate in her ears even after she opened her eyes.

She and Dr. Lenar had discussed the dream in previous sessions, and the doctor always said the same thing—that it was "a manifestation of the guilt" she felt over not saving her partner and that she needed to forgive herself. "It wasn't your fault," she would say, "and revisiting the details of the case will help you to see that." This time, though, Dr. Lenar simply said, "I'm going to start you on Zoloft to help with the anxiety." She scribbled a prescription on her letterhead as she spoke. "How's the Lunesta working out?" She handed the scrip to Andy.

Andy shrugged. "Good, I guess." The new sleeping pills were helping. In fact, she found that she could fall asleep if she even laid her head on a pillow or on the back of a chair just to rest.

Dr. Lenar turned concerned eyes on her. "Is there anything you'd like to discuss today? Any new memories?"

Andy shook her head.

"Problems? Concerns?"

Jennifer immediately came to mind. Andy remembered waking in her bed, the woman's breasts on her back and her arms possessively circling Andy's middle. The room smelled of sex, raw and natural. One of Jennifer's hands was resting on her left breast. As her eyes fell on that hand, she felt herself grow aroused, imagining everywhere Jennifer's hands had been. Andy seriously considered confessing her tryst with the author and then remembered Lenar's warning. "You've undergone a lot of stresses these last two years," she had said. "Your partner's death, the breakup with Kirsten, even joining the FBI. You need to focus on your recovery. A new relationship can get in the way of that." How would Lenar react to the news about Jennifer? Andy swallowed hard. "No problems," she said.

* * *

Lexy and Anna had agreed to meet the following Saturday afternoon at a little Vietnamese restaurant that Lexy had chosen in the downtown area. She liked it there, even though she couldn't read the menu and was deathly afraid of inadvertently consuming squid, because from a certain table the street looked like it was straight out of Manhattan. She'd always wanted to live there.

Lexy sat at that table, sipping her mineral water and waiting for her lunch companion to arrive. As she glanced at the faces of the other restaurant patrons, she felt a nagging fear that she might be recognized. What if a group of OCC instructors had lunch at this particular restaurant today and recognized Anna from one of their courses? What would they think of her?

She remembered stories quietly exchanged at college holiday parties or department meetings, behind the shield of someone's hand, about so-and-so and his young student. *The pig!* they'd say. *The cradle robber! Can't he find a woman his own age?* Lexy couldn't help but feel ashamed. What was she doing here? What good could come of this? Was she incapable of controlling her emotions? Was it even emotions or was it just lust, pure and simple?

She felt a sudden pang of guilt as she remembered a conversation she and Jules had had while lounging on the couch one evening.

"Someone younger will come along and turn your head," Jules had said.

"What? What are you talking about?" Lexy was only half listening as she made a note about sentence structure in the margin of a student's essay.

"Like her."

"Who?" Lexy looked up. On the television, an Olympic swimmer was bending slightly at the waist to allow a short man in a suit to place the medal around her neck. "Well, she is pretty toned."

Jules pinched her arm. "I'm serious," she said.

Lexy turned to face her. She took her hand. "I swear to you, no younger woman will ever turn my head away from you."

As if the universe were mocking her, just then Anna materialized on the street outside. And she looked beautiful. Her long, thick, wavy black hair fell softly and naturally over her shoulders, and she was wearing a vanilla V-neck top and fitted jeans. Lexy watched as she looked down at a piece of crumpled paper in her hand and up at the sign above the door. She then peered through the restaurant window, shielding her eyes from the sun with a hand and smiling broadly when she spotted Lexy.

Anna took the chair opposite her. "You look nice," she said.

Lexy blushed, her body once again seeming to lose contact with her mind. As she pondered the mind-body disconnect, she remembered a trip she once took to a psychic. She'd never really believed that someone could tell her future from picking cards from a deck, reading the creases in her palm or gazing into a glass ball, but she visited one once, dragged against her will by her college girlfriend, who believed in that stuff, that and the power of wheat germ.

The psychic had told Lexy that she was all head and no heart. She suggested that Lexy take up a physical activity as a means of emotional release, or, as she put it, a way to get her head and her heart "to at least wave at each other."

"I do cardio on the elliptical," Lexy said.

The woman smiled apologetically. "Sweetie, that's not gonna help, because for you that's a mental activity. You're counting time by calories. You've got to let yourself feel *without* thinking."

Grasping at straws, Lexy said, "I paint too."

The woman laughed in response and in between cackles retorted, "Your art lacks substance because you're not in touch with your own emotions. It's two-dimensional—an exercise in technique, not a practice of the heart."

Sculptures weren't two-dimensional, of course, but solid structures with even a moderate thickness had to be hollowed out to lessen the stress on the clay during drying or firing. She'd scraped out one just the other day to keep it from cracking. Were her sculptures emotional or were they hollow in that regard too? Perhaps the psychic was right. Maybe she was still struggling with getting her head and heart to wave at each other. She thought back to the sculpture that she'd just hollowed out. What was it that had moved her fingers, had compelled her to fashion Anna out of the clay? Was it her heart?

"So," Anna said, placing her keys and cell phone on the empty chair to her right, "I've been thinking about our grocery store rendezvous. I was curious what aisle we were in."

"Um..." Lexy had no idea. "I don't know. Frozen foods maybe. Why?"

"Well," Anna opened her menu, "if this were a novel, my literature professor would say that you must subconsciously associate me with the foods you envision in the aisle." Her eyes rolled up, capturing Lexy's. "Clearly, you see me as cold and frigid."

Lexy couldn't help but laugh. "What aisle did *you* have us in?"

Anna considered this for a moment. "I was thinking spicy— so the condiments aisle."

"I should have guessed."

After ordering, they fell into an easy and comfortable conversation. Anna talked about missing her mother, it having been almost a year since her passing, and Lexy was touched by the strong familial bond they obviously had shared. Lexy confessed her fear of public speaking and the debacle at the University of Southern Maine, her first experience in front of a classroom as a teaching assistant.

After the food arrived, the conversation somehow shifted to past relationships.

"Haley wanted me to move my mother into an assisted living facility or a convalescent home." Anna sipped her soda through her straw. "Can you believe that?"

"So what happened to Haley?"

"She eventually fell for one of our mutual friends. As far as I know they're still living together in Tallahassee."

Lexy couldn't understand how anyone would let a woman like Anna go. "Isn't it disturbing how some lesbians cycle through their circle of friends like that?"

Lexy noticed a touch of sauce on Anna's cheek and, without thinking, reached over to wipe it off.

Their eyes met and Lexy felt the hair on her arms stand on end. What was it about this woman?

Anna was the one who looked away this time, and when she did, Lexy released the breath she had been holding. She sat there, fighting an intense attraction to the woman sitting across from her, one of her students, and brimming with self-revulsion. She wanted to bury herself in her Bún bò Huế.

"How many relationships have you had?"

"Only three serious ones. In college, there was Shelby and Liana, and...I met Jules in graduate school." As usual, just saying her name caused tears to threaten.

"What's the matter?" Anna asked.

"I lost Jules to cancer four years ago. We were together eight years."

Anna placed her hand on Lexy's knee under the table. "I'm so sorry."

"It was a long time ago, but it still feels..."

"What a terrible thing to happen. I understand. I have the same trouble when people ask about my mom."

Somehow, in that moment, with thoughts of Jules in her head, the scene looked less like Manhattan and more like Florida; the palm trees in the background became visible and Lexy began to subconsciously count the number of pickup trucks, not cabs, that passed by the little restaurant window.

The waitress appeared and, perhaps sensing the seriousness of the conversation, placed the bill on the table and made a fast retreat.

Anna picked up the check.

Lexy immediately snatched it out of her hands. "I've got this," she said.

"Don't be silly." Anna took hold of the check and pulled it forcefully from Lexy's grasp.

"Anna, let me get it."

"*No!*" she said. "I've got it."

"Okay," Lexy smiled, "but I'll get it next time." Would there be a next time? Should there be?

# CHAPTER NINE

Officers Brenda Michaels and Rick Sterling of the Key West Police Department entered the main lobby of the Blue Parrot Apartment Complex.

Since no clerk was evident, they rang the bell.

A heavyset African-American woman in an extremely low-cut blouse took in Brenda Michaels's uniform as she positioned herself behind the counter.

"I thought you guys were finished asking questions here," she said, eyeing the notepad in the female officer's hand.

Officer Michaels read the nametag pinned to her blouse. "Adalia Johnson?" The woman nodded. "This is Officer Sterling and I'm Officer Michaels. If you have a few moments, we'd like to ask you some questions." Seeing Rick Sterling's eyes fall to the woman's cleavage, Michaels elbowed him in the ribs.

"'kay, but I only got a few minutes."

"This won't take long. You were the one on duty when the incident happened. Correct?"

"Yeah, that's right." Adalia Johnson chewed on her bottom lip, looking impatient.

"And you were also the one to answer Agent Cole's questions that day?"

"Yeah. Look, I already talked to the other guys." A pinprick of blood surfaced on the now-exposed skin of her lip.

Officer Michaels could tell from the woman's fidgety eyes that she was nervous about something.

"We just wanted to verify a few details with you. Agent Cole noted that she spoke with an Adalia Johnson a little after four thirty p.m. on Saturday, September fifth. Does that time sound about right?"

"I think so, but I didn't look at my watch."

"And you gave her the apartment number of a Mr. Creighton at that time?"

"Yeah, I guess so."

The noncommittal answers, and the woman's refusal to make eye contact, caused Michaels to grow suspicious. "Can you tell me what Agent Cole looked like?"

"What?" the woman stammered.

"Can you describe Agent Cole's appearance for us, please?"

The woman glanced at her watch. "Look, I've gotta go."

"Was she tall?"

"Um..."

"African-American? Caucasian? Hispanic?"

"I'm not...I see a lot of people..."

"Surely, Ms. Johnson, you must have noticed something about Agent Cole." Officer Michaels saw dots of perspiration gather on the woman's upper lip. "Was she in a uniform like us?"

"I'm sorry, but I don't remember."

As soon as Adalia heard the door of the police cruiser slam shut, her fingers began dialing.

The voice mail picked up.

"It's Dolly. We got a problem," she whispered into the phone. "Meet me at the pier when I get off."

* * *

Red Mohawk leaned his chair back so that it was balancing on two legs. "So what's so special about this guy?" he asked.

"Unlike the authors we've been discussing, Faulkner wasn't formally educated. But even though he dropped out of high school in December of his final year and lived in the poorest state in the nation, he went on to win the Nobel Prize." Lexy turned back to the PowerPoint slide projected onto the classroom's Smart Board and pointed to the picture in the collage of Faulkner in a tuxedo. "You can see him here accepting the prize in 1950."

A young woman glanced at the open book on the desk before her and asked, "This story's set during the Depression, right?"

"It was published a year after the stock market crash, but it was actually set during the Reconstruction Period in the post-Civil War South. How do we know that? What details in the story reveal the time period?" No hands went up. "When the narrator comments that Miss Emily's house was built in the seventies, is he or she referring to the Bee Gees and lava lamps time period?" There were a few laughs. "The architecture, with its scrolled balconies and cupolas, makes it sound almost like a plantation, right? When was the Civil War?"

"The 1950s?" a male student wearing a football jersey suggested tentatively.

"You're such an idiot!" A young blond woman in blue medical scrubs, fresh from her day job as a patient-care technician at the hospital, rolled her eyes dramatically. "You're only a century off, Einstein."

"From 1861 to 1865," Lexy announced, writing the dates on the board. "Faulkner hadn't even been born yet." Anytime there was a date, she felt the need to write it down. Not that she ever tested her students on such trivial things, but her own grade school teachers had put so much emphasis on dates—the dates of conquests, treaties and important events in history—that she had trouble ridding herself of the habit. "And some of the men in the town that attend Emily's funeral wear their old

Confederate uniforms. Those guys would be mummified by the 1970s."

"Okay, Dr. Strayer, but there's something I don't understand," said a girl who sat two seats away from the guy in the football jersey. "Why don't they suspect that she killed Homer? I mean, there's the poison-buying episode, and then the guy disappears."

"Well, let's look at how she's treated by the townspeople." Lexy opened her book and riffled through the pages of the story, which were marked up with margin notes and underlining. Finding the section she wanted, she placed her finger there. "When she buys the poison, she just walks right in there and demands arsenic, which would be the equivalent of me walking into CVS and demanding Vicodin. 'Gimme some Vicodin!' I say to the clerk. 'Um, ma'am, the law requires that you show us a physician's prescription.'" Reading from the text, she continued, "Do you think if I just stared down the clerk, my 'face like a strained flag'"—she looked up again—"that he'd run in the back and bag some up for me?" The class broke out in laughter.

"Of course not, he'd be dialing the cops to have the crazy woman arrested. But that's exactly what the druggist does for Emily even when she refuses to tell him what it's for." Lexy closed the book. "And what about the rotting corpse smell that's so bad that people complain to the Board of Aldermen? What do they do about that?"

"They sneak around her house in ski masks spreading lime," Red Mohawk said, still leaning back in his chair. Lexy was nervous that he was going to fall.

"Well, I don't know about the ski masks, but yes, they do spread lime around the perimeter of her house. And I'm pretty sure that if you or I had a similar smell emanating from our house, we'd have police at our door demanding entry with a warrant." Lexy said this while walking through the middle aisle until she arrived at Red Mohawk's desk. She pushed his chair down forcefully so that all four legs were on the floor, which caused the girl seated next to him to giggle.

"And the taxes, we didn't even mention the fact that they remitted her taxes from the time of her father's death because they felt bad that he left her nothing but the house. When my father died, the IRS didn't tell me to stop paying *my* taxes. So why," Lexy asked returning to the front of the room, "do the townspeople do these things? Why do they let all these things go? Why don't they put two and two together and figure out that the rotting corpse smell is probably Homer since Emily had recently purchased the poison and they saw the guy enter the house and never saw him again?"

Juan, a boy in the back row, offered, "Maybe they felt sorry for Emily?"

"Well, that's true. They do say 'Poor Emily' a number of times in the story. And why do they feel sorry for her?"

"Her father chased away all of her suitors, so she was left an old maid," the nontraditional student with the buzz cut answered.

Lexy was looking for a different answer, but she smiled anyway. "She is thirty and unmarried when her father dies."

"No one would want her then!" Red Mohawk's outburst was met with laughter.

"Women in their thirties can still be incredibly sexy," Anna offered, generating a nervous smile from Lexy.

"But it's got to be more than sympathy here. Remember that the pre-Civil War South was a system of elitism. You were important if you owned a plantation, if you had the right last name. And Emily is a Grierson, the last of the Griersons, in fact." Lexy sat on her desk and crossed one leg over the other.

"I get it. So Emily's sort of a symbol of the South?"

"Many critics think so. You could see her as the last vestige of the Old South. So it makes sense that she's so stubborn and resistant to change. Consider the mentality of the Southerners after the North burnt down their plantations."

Seeing the blank expressions on her students' faces, Lexy asked, "Remember *Gone with the Wind*?" No response. Perhaps they'd never seen *Gone with the Wind*. Lexy was always amazed by how quickly her references became outdated. "Think about the industrialism Northerners brought with them, the railroads, the gasoline pumps. Southerners liked things the way they were. They were stubborn and resistant just like Emily." Lexy took a sip of the tea in her travel mug. "We even see her stubbornness reflected in the incredibly dusty house, which Emily seems to have stopped caring for decades ago, and in her physical appearance. She's described as looking like a body long submerged in stagnant water. Have you guys seen *CSI*? This is not a pretty picture." A few laughs erupted.

"So what's with the title? If she's so horrible, if the South was so horrible, why give her a rose?" Juan asked, snapping his gum. Lexy was impressed with the question and smiled broadly.

"That's an excellent question, Juan. In fact, that's your homework over the weekend." A chorus of groans broke out. "Write me an essay explaining what you think the title means."

As the students filed out of the classroom, Lexy clicked off the projector and began fiddling with the computer, shutting it down. She saw in her peripheral vision that Anna was remaining seated. Lexy waited until all of the other students were gone to look at her. When she did, she was struck by how sexy she looked, chewing on her pen cap and staring at Lexy. Neither one spoke. Lexy glanced nervously at the open classroom door and at the faces of students and instructors as they walked by.

Anna wrote something down on a piece of notebook paper with her blue gel pen and folded inside it something from the front pouch of her backpack. She then grabbed her bag, slung it over her shoulder and walked toward Lexy's desk. The fluttery feeling in her stomach grew as the younger woman neared her. She wasn't sure what she would do if Anna touched her right then. She didn't know if she could resist or stop her. But Anna didn't touch her. *Thank god*, Lexy thought. Instead, she dropped the folded paper on the desk and silently left the room.

Lexy waited until she was safely in her office to open it. A ticket was inside. It was for Massenet's *Werther*, the opera at the Performing Arts Center. The note read: "It's not the frozen food aisle, but it'll have to do." Lexy smiled, placing the note and the ticket in the pocket of her trousers. She secretly liked having something that Anna had written so close to her skin. In fact, for the rest of the afternoon as she tried to focus on lesson plans and grading, her hand seemed to gravitate there, feeling for Anna's words in her pocket.

* * *

As Andy felt Jennifer pull away, she reached for her, trying to keep her in the warm bed for a little while longer. She fondled her breast in an attempt to convince her to stay, but Jennifer pushed her hand away.

"No more," she said adamantly. "We've *got* to join the living." She rolled away from Andy, who felt the loss instantly. "We should have dinner or go to a movie or something that involves clothing," she said.

Andy imagined the two of them at a restaurant together. Candlelight, good wine and stringed instruments. But the romantic image was immediately dispelled when she thought of the other restaurant patrons. What if a local cop recognized her and came up to chat or someone saw her wining and dining a suspect? "I don't think it's a good idea if anyone knows about us."

"Why the hell not?" Jennifer picked up her shirt off the floor and pulled it on over her head, as if suddenly aware of her nakedness.

Andy thought quickly. "The college."

"What about it?"

"Well, I'm new and I don't want to screw up my chances of landing a tenure-track position."

Jennifer sat down on the bed beside Andy and smoothed her hair back. "Sweetie, someone would have to retire or die in order for a position to open. You've read the memos about the budget."

"Well, Belman's gonna leave at some point. I hear the man's almost a corpse." Andy liked the comforting feel of Jennifer stroking her hair. Somehow it felt familiar, as though she'd been in this exact position before. For a moment she wished that she *was* a professor, that there was nothing besides this. She closed her eyes and imagined the sun on her face and the sound of ocean waves lapping on the shore. She almost drifted off. The sleeping pills were a little too helpful, she thought.

"Maybe something will open up." Andy could feel the bedsprings release, as Jennifer stood up. "We'll keep it quiet if you want. Besides, secret affairs are sexy," she purred.

From the bathroom, Jennifer yelled, "Do you want to join me in the shower?"

Andy spied what looked to be a quarter-inch-thick pile of paper fastened with binder clips on the maple bureau, half concealed by a newspaper. "No, I'm gonna rest for a little," she answered as she walked over to see what it was.

The top page read: "*Deadly Martini* by J. Deveaux." *The new manuscript.* Andy quickly began turning pages.

She had read to the end of Chapter Two by the time she heard Jennifer shut the water off.

Even though the murder hadn't yet happened, Andy could already guess, having read the other three books and beginning to understand the formulaic nature of Jennifer's work, which character would turn out to be the victim: a bartender named Angie. She had plenty of time, though, to figure out who the real Angie was since *Deadly Martini* wouldn't be hitting the bookshelves anytime soon. If some obsessed fan were responsible for the murders, as Andy theorized, he would lay low for a while waiting for book four's release, which would give them more time to sort through the evidence they'd already collected.

\* \* \*

Anna was walking Ginger around the lake when she was almost sideswiped by a dark-haired butch who was pounding along the sidewalk in gray sweats.

"Good grief!" she shouted, struggling not to lose her balance.

The woman didn't stop but barked a quick, "Watch where you're going!" as she passed.

Anna leaned down to pet Ginger, whom she had almost strangled with the leash when she yanked it hard in the process of trying not to fall. "Did that big bad woman scare you?" she asked as she patted the soft reddish-gold fur on Ginger's back. Ginger wagged her tail in response.

Anna found a shaded grassy area under a large oak and sat down to watch the swan paddleboats make their way across the murky water.

Ginger nudged at the backpack, knowing that the Frisbee was inside, and yipped.

"Okay, girl." Anna tousled the fur on Ginger's head with her fingers and then rummaged through the bag for the toy.

She threw the Frisbee hard with a flick of her wrist and watched Ginger leap into action, bounding through the high weeds toward the flying disc.

Ginger, the Frisbee between her teeth, returned before Anna even had a chance to flip open her sketchpad to the charcoal drawing she had started that morning. She tried to take the Frisbee from Ginger's mouth, but the dog turned away as she always did, wanting Anna to chase her for it. "Drop it," Anna commanded in a deep voice. Ginger continued to taunt her by coming closer and then pivoting away before she could snatch it. When Anna finally did manage to wrap her fingers around it, Ginger pulled the plastic toy in response, her teeth clamping down hard on its already chewed surface. "Drop it!" Anna instructed. Finally Ginger conceded. She looked up at her owner expectantly, wagging her tail.

Anna threw the disc again, farther this time, and returned to her sketchpad. She opened it right to the page she wanted and stared at the new portrait. It was Lexy again. She had been drawing Lexy since that first meeting at the vending machine— in class on her notebook paper, at home in her sketchpad. In fact, there was rarely a time in her day when the woman was absent from her thoughts.

She thought of the opera ticket now, wondering if Lexy would show. She'd used her rainy day fund, plus that week's tips, to buy a long, satin, strapless number that she looked fantastic in. The shape was flattering, with darting at the bust, and the color was a soft brown that made Anna think of Lexy's eyes.

She'd never been to an opera before. She picked this particular one because she'd read the German novella on which it was based, *The Sorrows of Young Werther* by Johann Wolfgang von Goethe. The story was a terribly sad one about Werther, a young poet, and his desperate love for a woman named Charlotte. Charlotte marries another man. Although she eventually does confess her love for Werther, by then it's too late. The young poet has already taken his life. It wasn't too late for her own confession, though, she thought.

Anna was filling in the shadow along Lexy's cheekbone with her pencil when she felt Ginger's wet nose on her thigh. This time Ginger willingly surrendered the Frisbee and Anna obliged by whipping it across the field.

* * *

Andy stopped her morning jog to answer her cell. Every morning since graduating from The Citadel, aside from a few weeks following Seth's death, she ran at least two miles.

Out of breath, she grumbled into the mouthpiece, "Cole here."

"Key West PD brought in Adalia Johnson, the hotel clerk at the Blue Parrot, for questioning, and unearthed some pretty interesting stuff." Reilly's voice sounded unusually excited.

"Yeah? Like what?" Andy was still struggling to catch her breath. Placing her hands on her knees, she bent over at the waist.

"She's got a rap sheet—drugs mostly and petty theft, but they've pinned felony charges on her and her boyfriend, a fisherman named Jo Jo, for an illegal gun-running operation. They think she's got information on the Jensen girl. They're gonna try to strike up a deal."

"That's great," Andy said, feeling a muscle cramp beginning in her left calf. "Anything else?"

"Yeah, get this: She's *not* the Adalia Johnson you spoke to."

"What?" Andy massaged her calf muscle through the leg of her sweatpants.

"Her cousin..." She could hear Reilly shuffle some papers. "A woman named Vertice Brown was covering for Ms. Johnson at the time you arrived at the Blue Parrot so that she could slip away to have a little rendezvous with Jo Jo. Obviously the real Adalia Johnson didn't come forward before because of either her involvement with this nefarious Jo Jo character or her fear of losing her job. They're calling in the cousin for questioning."

*The plot thickens*, Andy thought.

\* \* \*

Lexy was surprised to get Rand's call requesting her presence at his and Ari's Fifties Television Theme Night, given the slumber party she'd had only two weeks earlier with Audrey Hepburn, George Peppard and a sobbing Rand.

"I'm going to be Lucy!" his giddy voice shrieked into the phone. Lexy could imagine him twirling around the kitchen like a ballerina.

"So I guess I'm to assume that you and Ari have made up?"

"Old news." Rand sounded incredibly chipper. "I thought pot roast and baby carrots for dinner. What do ya think?"

"I'll probably be a wet rag, Daddy-O," Lexy said.

"You just get your classy chassis over here next Friday! And bring a hot squeeze." With that, he hung up.

\* \* \*

In the cafeteria Thursday morning, Lexy eyed Jennifer, who was busy calculating grades, her eyebrows bunched together in consternation. She wondered what Jennifer would look like with a greasepaint mustache like Groucho Marx's.

"My neighbor's having a party a week from Friday, and I thought maybe you'd—"

"You made me mess up! Now I've got to add all of this together again!" Jennifer sighed loudly, throwing her calculator down on the table.

"It's a theme party—1950s television." Lexy gave Jennifer the best puppy dog face she could. "Want to be my date?"

"Why don't you ask your little hussy student?" Jennifer scowled and punched a few of the calculator's buttons with the back of her Bic pen.

"That was rude! She's not a hussy!" Sometimes Lexy wondered about her friendship with Jennifer—whether it was based on convenience, the fact that they both worked in the same college, or a real connection.

"Well, that's for sure. You're certainly not gonna get anything out of that virginal chick!"

"What the hell's your problem?"

"Just kidding. Gosh, take a Midol! Don't get your panties all in a wad, okay?" She tapped her pen against her chin. "Let's see, fifties television, huh? Wasn't *Zorro* on then?"

"I have no idea. Rand and his boyfriend are going to be Lucy and Ricky."

Jennifer framed Lexy's face with her fingers and squinted one eye like a director filming a scene. "With a mustache, you could be the *Have Gun Will Travel* guy," Jennifer mused.

"Thanks a lot." Lexy rolled her eyes.

* * *

On Saturday evening, Anna stared at the high, vaulted ceiling of the Performing Arts Center. Her eyes took in the white birch timber and the garishly decorated upper balconies. She couldn't help but anxiously look over at the empty seat next to her. *She's not coming*, she thought to herself, and she could feel a lump begin to form in her throat. It was just as the lights dimmed to alert the patrons to be seated that she spotted her. An usher with a small pen flashlight was directing her to the row.

Suddenly, she couldn't breathe. Lexy was wearing a silk charmeuse gown with a V-neck bodice and ruched bust. Although her hair was pulled back in a French twist, showing off her slender neck and dangling earrings, some hair hung loosely and framed her face. Unable to take her eyes off her, Anna watched as the others seated in Row F pulled their knees in or stood to allow her to pass.

"I didn't think you were coming," Anna said, finally finding her voice.

Lexy took in Anna's dress. "Lovely," she said. And then the lights dimmed for a final time.

\* \* \*

Lexy was uncharacteristically late to the opera because she had spent twenty minutes pacing outside the PAC, deciding whether or not to go in. Jules, who never cared what other people thought, lived by her principles alone and Lexy had adored her for that. Unfortunately, Lexy had never felt comfortable enough with herself to lead quite so authentic a life. She made decisions based on how those decisions would be perceived by others, sometimes even by strangers. And here she was—deciding whether to hurt Anna or to risk being the brunt of someone's bad joke or the focus of some piece of juicy gossip. Jules would be disappointed in her and maybe even call her a coward if she left. So she didn't.

Even in the dark, though, Lexy couldn't help but glance around them, worrying that one of her superiors, colleagues or, even worse, students would recognize them. How would she explain what she was doing at the opera in an evening gown with her student?

At some point during the performance, Lexy forgot completely about her fears that they would be discovered and fell victim to young Werther's tragic story. She didn't know when she had started crying but she suddenly could taste the salty tears on her lips. She couldn't understand the French words, but she could *feel* the emotion in the notes as the characters sang.

Anna, perhaps sensing Lexy's sadness, reached over and laced her fingers in hers. Lexy didn't pull away but rather continued to hold her hand in her lap for the remainder of Act IV.

Anna had parked on the street a couple blocks from the PAC, but they had to wait for Lexy's car to be brought around by the valet.

"It's only ten," Anna said, checking her watch. "We could have a drink somewhere."

"Dressed like this?" Lexy looked down at her gown.

"I have a bottle of French wine I've been waiting to open. And it just so happens," Anna smiled coyly, "that you're dressed perfectly for the Chateau de Anna."

Lexy laughed. "I should probably get home."

"One drink?" Anna pushed her bottom lip forward in a pout, which Lexy found totally irresistible.

"Only one."

"Agreed."

\* \* \*

Anna's one-bedroom apartment was located above a garage connected by a covered walkway to a 1930s bungalow-style house. Her elderly landlady, Mrs. Cortenza, charged her a more than reasonable rent and in exchange Anna helped with odd jobs around the house and in the yard.

As Anna unlocked the side door and led Lexy up the narrow steps, she wondered how her professor would view her apartment. Someone in her late twenties should be more established than this, she thought, as she opened the door and gestured her in. She directed Lexy to the kitchen, which had high stools and a bar off the island, but no table.

Lexy took a seat on one of the stools while Anna rummaged through a hutch with a built-in wine rack. "Here it is!" she said, emerging with a bottle of red wine.

Anna clinked her glass with Lexy's. They both took a sip.

"Thank you for tonight," Lexy said.

Anna remained standing, a bit afraid of sitting so close to Lexy on the other barstool. "My pleasure," she said, sipping her wine. "What did you think of the opera?"

"Such a sad story! But beautiful. Absolutely beautiful."

"I thought so too." Anna wondered what the fabric of Lexy's silky dress would feel like in her fingers. "So, why don't you tell me something I don't know about you?"

"Like what?"

"Like…" What Anna really wanted to know was if Lexy liked holding her hand at the opera as much as she did. Knowing she couldn't ask that question, she ventured, "Like when you knew you were gay."

\* \* \*

Lexy took a sip of her wine. "I think I've always known. I never really had any significant relationships with men." Her mind conjured up the image of a young fourteen-year-old girl with freckles and strawberry-blond hair. "It was junior high school when I had my first real crush. She was my best friend. We had grown up together. I remember when we were really little we used to pretend to smoke cigarettes. Remember those candy cigarettes?" Anna nodded. "And we'd sit on her older brother Danny's motorcycle and pretend we were cool."

"I bet you *were* cool." Anna smiled.

"Well, I don't know about that. But Laura…my god, I haven't thought about her in forever." Lexy felt a smile spread across her face as she revisited the memory. "She was my first kiss. It was so soft." Her fingers went to her lips, and she grew aroused as she imagined Anna kissing her there. "It never felt that way with boys. Like silk."

Lexy felt a slight buzz from the wine. She looked at Anna, who was still standing. "Why don't you sit down?" Lexy patted the stool next to her own.

Anna moved closer but didn't sit. Lexy watched the younger woman's eyes fall to her V-neck bodice.

"You know, maybe I should get going?"

"Don't go," Anna pleaded. Her voice sounded desperate.

"Yeah, I really should. I want to get to the Community Center early tomorrow and—"

Without warning, Lexy felt Anna's hand softly caress the back of her neck. "Please, don't go," she said again.

Lexy couldn't relax. Her skin was aflame, her body thrumming with desire. She was Anna's teacher. She couldn't cross that line. She *wouldn't* cross that line. "I can't," she said, violently pushing her hand away.

"I'm falling for you."

"Don't." Lexy stood, thinking if she could put space between them, she could think more clearly and rein in her emotions.

"I can't help it." Anna moved toward her.

Lexy put her hand up to stop Anna from coming any closer. "Don't!" she said again.

Anna's fingers were trembling as she wrapped them around Lexy's outstretched hand, clearing the makeshift blockade. "Tell me you don't want this," she whispered, "and I'll stop." Lexy said nothing. Anna moved closer still so that they were almost touching.

"I want to kiss you," she breathed, inches away from Lexy's lips. "I've *wanted* to kiss you for weeks. And now, in that dress…" Her green eyes darkened with desire as she leaned toward Lexy.

Lexy wriggled away from her.

"I'm sorry," was all Lexy managed to say before she grabbed her keys off the counter and ran toward the door.

# CHAPTER TEN

A week had passed since the opera, and Lexy's life was beginning to get back to normal. She was putting the finishing touches on her outfit for Rand and Ari's '50s-themed party when Jennifer arrived.

Lexy laughed as she took in Jennifer's outfit. "Are those Underoos?"

"Faster than a speeding bullet! More powerful than a locomotive! Able to leap tall buildings in a single bound!"

Jennifer flared her red cape out with her hands. "You like?" she asked. Her hair was heavily gelled and pushed back off her face, and the light blue bodysuit she was wearing was padded, probably to make her appear muscular. It actually gave her the impression of being pudgy, like the Stay Puft Marshmallow Man. Over the skintight garment she wore red satin boxer shorts and a ridiculous plastic yellow belt. Her feet were shod in eighteen-hole oxblood Doc Martens boots.

"*Like* is a little strong," Lexy chuckled. "How'd I do?" Channeling her character, Lexy shoved her hands into the pockets of her charcoal men's slacks and slouched, touching the brim of the dark brown fedora that she'd found at the Salvation Army. A plain white T-shirt and striped, dark gray vest completed the outfit.

"Let me guess." Jennifer rapped lightly on Lexy's hat with her knuckles. "A lovable sewer worker, perhaps?"

"Hey, hey, Ralphie-boy!" Lexy would have tipped her hat, but she didn't want to have to mess with her hair again.

"So. Where's the party?"

Rand answered the door in a red wig, signature *I Love Lucy* lipstick, a black and white polka dot dress and white apron. He posed with one of his high-heeled feet pointed, his index finger, complete with painted artificial nail, placed on the side of his red mouth and his eyes rolled upward as if he were considering something. "Ricky!" he yelled, sounding almost exactly like Lucy aside from the fact that he was an octave or two off. "Norton and Superman have arrived!" He batted his fake eyelashes at the two costumed women in his doorway. "Do come in," he said, extending his arm into the crowded foyer.

Costumed guests, mostly men, stood in small groups, couples chatting with martini glasses and plastic plates overflowing with appetizers in their hands.

Ari, dressed in a shirt with Babalu sleeves, bow tie, cummerbund and black pants, emerged from the kitchen carrying a tray of deviled eggs. When he saw Jennifer, his mouth fell open and he dropped the tray on the condo's saltillo tile floor, making a paprika- and egg yolk-colored mess on it and on his shiny leather shoes.

"Dear Lord!" Rand spluttered, making his way over to his partner. "Ari, you look like you've seen a ghost!"

Ari said nothing. Rand disappeared behind the sliding French door that separated the dining area from the kitchen and reemerged in a few moments holding a roll of paper towels.

Ari didn't move but just stared like some plaster statue as Jennifer and Lexy made their way toward him through the throng of '50s TV stars that included Ed Sullivan, Mighty Mouse and the Lone Ranger.

"Someone has *got* to explain to me why he just called my publisher Ari!" Jennifer said. Lexy couldn't help but wonder how anyone could take her seriously in her sky-blue bodysuit.

"Isn't your brother a publisher?" Ed Sullivan asked Ari, setting his tinfoil microphone down on the dining table's red-checkered tablecloth. He bent down to help Rand clean up the mess.

"Let's go into the kitchen," Ari said to Jennifer, his eyes darting back and forth with the alacrity of a tennis ball in a match at Wimbledon.

Rand clearly had had too much to drink. Lexy watched as he stole an olive on a toothpick from the Lone Ranger's dirty martini and tried, sloppily, to use the stick to show the cowboy how deep his throat was. Lexy cringed and sipped her Appletini. She was searching the crowd for a distraction when Ari and Jennifer reemerged from the kitchen. Jennifer was looking decidedly confused and exhausted.

Rand pulled at the Lone Ranger's gun belt, almost causing the mustached man to fall toward him, and then drunkenly slurred, "My, what a big gun you have!"

Ari made his way quickly through the crowd and grabbed Rand's wrist, yanking his hand away from the other man's belt buckle.

Imitating Ricky Ricardo, Ari said, "Lucy, you have some splainin' to do. You've had too much to drink." He whispered this last part quietly but sternly through his teeth. Gesturing to the Lone Ranger apologetically, he steered Rand toward the kitchen.

"What happened with Ari in the kitchen?"

Jennifer shook her head. "Things are not as they seem, my friend. Not at all. Could it be that we're in one of Shakespeare's comedies?" Taking in their costumes, she added, "We're dressed perfectly for the part."

The sound of glass breaking followed by Rand's distinctive voice screaming something incoherent pulled the women's attention toward the kitchen. They raised their eyebrows at each other in surprise.

Ed Sullivan gallantly announced, "I'll go in and see if they need any help."

When the door opened, Lexy could hear Rand shout, "Great! Another of Ricky's romps! You're such a man-whore!"

Jennifer set her drink down so hard that it splashed onto the tabletop. "This is ridiculous! This is supposed to be a party!" Mumbling the word "faggots" under her breath, she stormed toward the kitchen.

Lexy was horrified. Jennifer was dressed as a hero, but Lexy knew somehow that she was going to do more harm than good.

\* \* \*

Jennifer burst into the kitchen like a cowboy entering a saloon.

"Look, Lucy, it's the fifties here tonight. Boys will be boys!" she shouted. "Who cares if he's a fucking man-whore! Maybe you should have been Elizabeth Taylor instead."

Rand's jaw dropped, and Ed made a fast retreat to the living room.

Ari frowned. "Ms. Gardiner, *please*, this really isn't any of your business."

Jennifer fluffed her cape. "Well, publishing isn't your business, but that didn't stop you!"

"Look, Super Dyke," Rand said, "you're a guest at this party, and you need to be respectful of my husband." Both men stared at each other, the anger melting from their eyes.

Rand pulled Ari toward him by his tie. "Oh, Ricky, you're wonderful! I would never have you deported!"

\* \* \*

On Wednesday of the following week, Lexy taught a lesson on T.S. Eliot.

"In lines seventy-three and seventy-four, Prufrock claims that he should have been 'a pair of ragged claws scuttling across the floors of silent seas.'" Lexy sipped coffee from her travel mug and, finding it cold, grimaced. "What kind of creature is he describing?"

A usually quiet student named Robert answered, "A crab."

"And someone tell me how a crab walks."

"Side to side." Jenna, the bottle-blond, dual-enrollment student, moved her pink highlighter back and forth like a pendulum for emphasis.

"Yes, and why would Prufrock, the speaker of this poem, say that he should have been a crab?" Lexy waited for signs of recognition in the twenty sets of eyes before her.

"Because he's a coward!" For the first time in two weeks, Anna spoke. "He spends his whole life paralyzed by the fear of rejection, going back and forth in his head like a crab. He never actually makes a move forward. He never approaches the women."

Although startled, Lexy nodded at her approvingly. "Yes! He's incredibly indecisive. He's worried that the women will notice his balding head and thinning frame, and they'll 'fix him in a formulated phrase'—old balding guy, perhaps." A few students chuckled.

"Despite Ezra Pound's insistence on leaving out the reference," Lexy continued, "Hamlet actually works very well here since Hamlet is indecisive too—'To be or not to be,' right?" A few students laughed. "Prufrock, however, is *not* Prince Hamlet, he tells us. Remember that ultimately Hamlet does decide to kill his uncle after his reaction to the play proves his guilt. But Prufrock only wonders if he should dare to disturb the universe."

"Prufrock *should* have disturbed the universe," Anna said abruptly, startling Lexy.

"Yes, I suppose he should have, because then his moments of greatness might not have just flickered and gone out. So why," Lexy asked, "is this called 'The Love Song'? Where is the *love* in this poem?"

Lexy waited and, seeing a few students fidget uncomfortably, decided to answer her own question. "There is no love for J. Alfred Prufrock because he never risked anything, and love requires risk, doesn't it?" Lexy's eyes traveled the room as they normally did while she taught. "*Carpe diem*," she said. "That would be Prufrock's message. He would tell you to disturb the universe in all kinds of wonderful ways." As she scanned the room, Lexy glimpsed Anna's green eyes, which had turned watery.

"Although Prufrock was middle-aged, Eliot first published this poem in 1917." Lexy wrote the year on the board. "He was born in 1888. Where are the math majors?" A few hands went up. "Someone tell me how old he was when he first published this poem." Lexy waited, giving the students a few minutes to calculate.

Red Mohawk, who had surprised Lexy by being one of the better writers in the classroom, piped up, "Twenty-nine."

"Yes, and what's so special about being twenty-nine, folks?"

"He's almost thirty," said a male voice from the back of the room. "He's old!" That produced a number of chuckles.

"That's right. He's old, very, very old." Lexy laughed, thinking that Anna, almost the same age as Eliot when he published the poem, was nowhere near old. "Your homework for next Monday..." A few students groaned melodramatically. "...is to write me an essay explaining why you think Eliot would write this poem at that age."

Lexy watched as most of the students jotted a note about the assignment in their notebooks and began collecting their belongings off their desks and the floor.

"I'll see you all on Monday. Have a good weekend!"

"'Would it have been worth it,' Dr. Strayer, 'after the cups, the marmalade, the tea, among the porcelain, among some talk of you and me'?" Anna asked abruptly from the back of the room, her eyes brimming with tears. "'Would it have been worthwhile, to have bitten off the matter with a smile, to have squeezed the universe into a ball, to roll it towards some overwhelming question'?" The other students looked confused.

Lexy felt panicked. She wanted to run.

"That's not what you meant at all, is it, Dr. Strayer? 'That is not it, at all.'" Anna's voice sounded like a low growl.

Lexy was sweating. "Excuse me?"

Anna picked up her backpack, slung it over her shoulder and walked out of the classroom.

# CHAPTER ELEVEN

"I need a home address for this Arnold Flemming." Andy Cole clicked her pen impatiently. "I can't believe no one has questioned the publisher!"

"Well, apparently they called Flemming Press a number of times but haven't yet reached this Arnold character who's been handling Gardiner's contract since the release of *Icy Waters*. They spoke with his brother each time." Reilly ran a quick search in the Florida driver's license database. "Here it is," he said. "Winter Haven, 2648 Green Lane."

"I'm on it," she said and hung up.

* * *

Andy parked her Jeep outside the Spanish-style town home on Green Lane in Winter Haven. There was no car in the driveway or in the garage, so she didn't expect anyone to answer when she rang the doorbell.

To her surprise, the door opened, revealing a short, round woman wearing a gray housekeeping tunic. In one hand she was holding a spray bottle containing a bright blue liquid and in the other a pink feather duster.

"I'm Agent Andrea Cole." Andy flipped open her badge ID case and held her FBI shield out for the woman to inspect. "I'm looking for Arnold Flemming. Is he here?"

"Señor Flemming?"

"Yes, Mr. Flemming. Is he here?" Andy looked past the woman and found a tastefully furnished foyer leading to what appeared to be a sitting room.

"Uh, no. Señor Flemming iss away." She had a thick Hispanic accent.

"Away where?" The woman looked up and to the right as if she were considering her answer carefully before speaking. "It's very important, Ms...."

"Sanchez."

"Ms. Sanchez, it's *very* important that we get in touch with Mr. Flemming."

She motioned Andy inside with her feather duster. "He's in California," she whispered as if there were others in the house with them.

"Where?"

The woman disappeared into the kitchen. When she returned a few moments later, she was holding open an address book and pointing at an entry on one of the pages. Andy read "Azure Acres Recovery Center."

"Drugs?"

"*Si*. He's been there *seis* months already."

"Thank you, Ms. Sanchez. You've been very helpful." Andy scribbled the name of the rehabilitation facility on her notepad.

She started dialing before she even made it to the car.

"Reilly." Her partner's voice sounded exhausted.

"It's Cole. I need you to check something out for me. Flemming's cleaning lady claims that he's been in the Azure Acres Recovery Center in California for six months. Can you verify that?"

"No problem." Reilly jotted the name down. "I'll have an answer for you by the end of today."

* * *

Anna was working on a paper on Homeland Security for her Government class when she heard a knock at her apartment door.

Through the peephole, she spied Mrs. Cortenza, who was shifting her weight from one foot to the other. She stopped and smiled with no teeth showing when Anna opened the door. "There's a gentleman here to see you," she said. "He's waiting in the foyer."

"What gentleman?"

"A Mr. Connors."

Anna didn't know any Mr. Connors. "Is he a salesman or something?"

"I'm sure I don't know, Dear."

Anna followed her landlady down the stairs to the main house. Mrs. Cortenza held the screen door open for her and motioned her in. A man wearing mirrored sunglasses and a navy suit and matching tie stood stiffly in the center of the living room. He looked like a Secret Service agent or a character from the *Matrix* movies. The straightness of his back made her uncomfortable; Anna wished that he would sit. In her periphery, she saw Mrs. Cortenza disappear into her kitchen.

"Ms. Anna Stevens?" the man asked.

"That's me." Anna didn't know why, but she was incredibly nervous. She wrung her hands together as she expected women did when uninvited army officials or policemen showed up at the front door of their homes. Perhaps it was all the Homeland Security articles she had been reading.

"I'm Patrick Connors, an attorney." He removed his glasses. The skin that surrounded his eyes was pale, and Anna wondered how often he wore them. "I've left several messages."

Anna felt in her pocket for her cell and then remembered that she'd plugged it in to charge the night before. Had it been on silent all night and all day?

"I'm afraid I have some bad news, Ms. Stevens." She stiffened. "My client, Mr. Ian Fenner, has been killed by a car bomb explosion in Tel Aviv."

"*Israel?* What?" She couldn't imagine Ian anywhere except Bethesda, Maryland.

"He was covering a story at the embassy."

"Oh my god!" Anna's hand covered her mouth. She felt as though she might be sick. "What? When did this happen?"

"Tuesday night." *Three days ago.*

"Why am I only now hearing about this?"

"I wasn't contacted until yesterday. And as I said, I've been trying to reach you."

"And Cayden? Where's Cayden? Was he with him?" Her stomach lurched.

"Cayden is fine." She breathed a sigh of relief. "As I'm sure you're aware, Ms. Stevens, Mr. Fenner had explicit instructions in his will about what was to be done with Cayden in the event of his death." Anna heard the words "guardianship," "legal papers" and "biological mother." Of course they'd talked about it. Ian had no family—his parents having disowned him shortly after learning that he was gay and his partner Christian having been killed in a drunk driving accident over a year ago. But Anna would have never imagined that there'd be a need for her to become Cayden's guardian—not when she'd signed the papers and not now.

She swallowed the lump in her throat as she remembered the day she had given birth to little Cayden. Ian and Christian were crowding her in the delivery room, anxious to see the cresting head of their little boy. She remembered how she had reached for him when the nurse picked him up off her stomach to place him in his daddy's arms for the first time. But then she also remembered how sweet it was, the way that Ian coddled the baby in his arms, the look of absolute devotion in his ocean-blue eyes. It was that look that had convinced her that she had done the right thing.

"Ma'am?" the attorney was saying.

"I'm sorry. I'm just...stunned, I guess."

"I was asking if you're ready for me to retrieve Cayden from the car."

Anna's eyes turned to the bay windows and to the black Peugeot SUV parked at the curb out front. "He's here?" she asked in a trembling voice. She hadn't seen Cayden in person since he was four weeks old, when Ian and Christian moved their family to Bethesda. She had memories of nursing him in her mother's rocking chair, the one that she herself had been nursed in. He was all wrapped up in a mint-green Winnie the Pooh blanket. The dark head of hair with which he had been born had poked out over the top of the blanket like a houseplant gone wild.

Every so often, Ian and Christian would send her an envelope that was marked "Do Not Crush" in red block letters. She loved seeing those red letters, because they meant that inside were photos of Cayden. They had decided early on that Cayden should know about her. She had sent Cayden gifts every birthday and holiday, and she talked to him on the phone—as much as someone could talk to an infant, anyway. On his fourth birthday, which had just passed, she had sent him a green stuffed dragon and a Gordon's Express Lego train set that Ian had told her he wanted.

"Yes. Ms. Stevens, would you like me to go get him?"

"I...I don't...Yes...Of course." She followed him through the screen door and then watched from the porch as he traveled the sidewalk to the SUV.

Connors pulled the back door open, giving Anna her first glimpse of the boy—tiny maroon Chuck Taylor sneakers, which swung out of the door before his body followed. He stood maybe three feet tall, and his hair was wavy and dark like Anna's. His eyes were green like Anna's. She recognized Ian in his chin and his smile. He was wearing a Teenage Mutant Ninja Turtles T-shirt and little khaki GAP shorts. In his arms was a green stuffed dragon. Anna immediately started crying.

She watched them come up the walk, Cayden's little fingers engulfed by Mr. Connors's hand, which, in comparison, appeared giant-sized like a catcher's mitt. The boy's eyes were fixed on the neighbor's yard, where an egret was picking at something in the grass. He pointed at the bird. "A seagull!" he said.

Mr. Connors smiled but didn't respond.

Cayden didn't actually look at her until he'd reached the front steps. But when he did, he clearly recognized her, wriggling free of Mr. Connors's hand and racing toward her like a freight train. His little arms wrapped around her legs. He smelled of crayons and Band-Aids.

"Do you know who I am?" she asked.

He giggled. "You're my mommy."

She wrapped her arms around him and pulled his tiny frame off the ground. "That's right," she said through streaming tears. "I'm your mommy."

\* \* \*

Andy Cole answered her cell by clicking a button on her Bluetooth earpiece.

"Cole here," she said gruffly.

"I verified the cleaning woman's statement. Arnold Flemming checked himself into the rehabilitation center in LA back in May."

"Can patients leave the center?"

"No. It's pretty much a locked-down facility." Dead end, Andy thought.

"Do we know who's been handling his accounts since he's been detoxing?"

"His twin brother—Ari Flemming."

"Does he have an alibi?"

"Nobody's officially questioned him yet."

"Let's have OCPD bring him in."

\* \* \*

Ari glanced at what his attorney, Douglas Flynn, was wearing: running pants and a T-shirt that said "Yale" on the front. Based on the darkened ring around Flynn's collar and the sweat circles under his arms, Ari guessed that the guy had been working out when he'd gotten the call to accompany him to the police station. Ari made a mental note to search Angie's List for a new lawyer. If he was going to be represented by someone, that someone should, at the very least, be well-dressed.

When the detective pressed a button on the recorder, Ari's heart raced. He could feel the perspiration on his palms.

"Please state your name, age and occupation for the record."

"Ari Flemming. Forty-nine. Accountant." The African-American detective interviewing him was decidedly attractive, Ari thought—clean-shaven, nicely dressed and muscular. Ari's eyes fell on the simple gold band on the ring finger of his left hand. *Damn!*

"Mr. Flemming, can you account for your whereabouts on September fifth between the hours of three p.m. and four p.m.?"

Ari fidgeted uncomfortably. Douglas nodded at him to continue. "I was in Key West."

"Can you be more specific, Mr. Flemming?"

"It was…um…three to four? Let's see." He scratched at his bald spot. "I was probably eating. We were having an early dinner at a restaurant."

"We?" the detective prompted.

"Is this really important, Detective Parker?"

"Mr. Flemming, may I remind you that a woman is dead? That the person who killed her may have killed two others and be planning more murders? Please answer the questions to the best of your ability. Who was with you?" Chase Parker seemed irritated by Ari's attorney, occasionally frowning in his direction. Ari could understand why. Douglas couldn't sit still. His right leg was shaking, and the friction produced by the sheer material of his running pants was yielding a funny swishing sound.

"Bradley Whittaker."

"And what relation is he to you?"

"Douglas?" Ari turned pleading eyes on his attorney.

"It's okay, Ari."

"Brad was a one-time affair," Ari explained. He had met him in an Internet chat room for forty-something gay men. They had been talking for maybe a month when Brad had suggested that they meet. Ari remembered staring at Brad's picture, wondering what he should do. He liked the attention, having not felt Rand's affection for some time. He had decided not to go but changed his mind at the last minute after he and Rand fought over laundry he had left in the washer overnight.

"In order to verify your whereabouts, we'll need to contact Mr. Whittaker." The detective's expression hadn't changed throughout the interview. He hadn't even batted an eyelash upon realizing that Ari was gay. "Do you recall the name of the restaurant, Mr. Flemming?"

Ari thought back to his fried shrimp platter. "Pisces," he said.

The interview continued for another twenty or so minutes, with the detective asking Ari all sorts of questions about his time in Key West, where he and Brad stayed, what beaches they went to. He also asked about Ari's relationship to Jennifer.

Douglas had encouraged him to tell the detective the truth about Arnold. "Ari, this is serious!" he had said before they walked into the station. "You're being questioned about a freakin' murder!"

"So let me understand," the detective massaged his forehead with his index and middle fingers. "Your twin brother, Arnold, Jennifer's publisher, checked himself into rehab, and you've been impersonating him so that he doesn't lose contracts? Is that right, Mr. Flemming?"

"Well, you see..." Ari knew it sounded crazy. "It's a family business. And we figured that his authors would find other publishers in the time that it took Arnold to recover."

"Couldn't you just have dealt with his clients as yourself—Arnold's brother?"

"I'm not a publisher, Detective Parker. I have no experience in publishing. And Flemming Press is a small company with few employees and few accounts."

The detective sipped his water bottle. "Just how many accounts is your brother currently responsible for?"

"Just three, including Ms. Gardiner's."

\* \* \*

Adalia Johnson's cousin, Vertice Brown, sat in the investigation room in the Key West Police Department waiting for Detective Bunson to return. The off-white walls looked tobacco-stained, and there were some ceiling tiles marred by water marks. One wall was all mirror. As she stared at her own reflection, she wondered if there were people watching her from the other side like in the police dramas she had seen on television. She wondered if the detective would offer her a cigarette or threaten her with force like on *Law and Order*.

Bunson had a bushy gray mustache that made Vertice think of a walrus. He was not dressed in a traditional police uniform but instead was wearing a stained yellow shirt, much in need of ironing, and brown slacks. His belly hung over his belt and hid the fly of his pants. Around his plump pink neck, he wore an ID badge on a chain. He smelled of stale cigarettes and perspiration. Vertice didn't like him.

Bunson pushed the record button on the digital recorder that sat on the table between them. Vertice thought his fat fingers looked like sausages.

"Mrs. Brown, based on your cousin's sworn statement, we have come to understand that you were manning the front desk in her place on September fifth from just before four p.m. until nine p.m. that evening. Is that correct?"

Vertice adjusted the collar of her shirt, which she noticed in the mirror was hanging funny. "Yeah, Officer, that's right."

"It's Detective, ma'am."

She rolled her eyes. "Yes, *Detective*."

Bunson sipped camel-colored coffee from a Styrofoam cup. Vertice couldn't help but stare at the droplets of coffee left in his wiry walrus mustache.

"Do you remember an Agent Cole questioning you that day?"

"Yes."

"And what time was that?"

"Let's see. Adalia left around three forty, and I was there almost an hour when the lady FBI agent came. I'd guess around four thirty."

"Four thirty p.m.?"

"Yeah."

"Did anyone else come in asking about Samantha Jensen?"

"No."

"Did you notice anything odd? Anyone lingering around the lobby or Mr. Creighton's apartment?"

Vertice shook her head.

"Is there anything at all that you remember about that day that might be pertinent to our investigation?"

Vertice thought back to that Saturday when the agent had showed her her silver badge. The woman's hair and clothes had been messy. Vertice remembered seeing her swipe at some red stains on her white sleeve as if she'd just realized that they were there. "You know, I did notice something strange."

"Yes?"

"She was wrinkled. Her clothes, I mean."

"Wrinkled?"

"And her shirt was stained. I didn't really think anything of it, but now that I'm remembering back, the sleeve of her shirt was dotted with something red and she was trying to, you know, wipe it off."

Bunson hit the Styrofoam cup with his arm, spilling coffee all over the table. He hurriedly picked up the legal notepad before it soaked up the coffee like a sponge. His eyebrows formed a V over the bridge of his nose and his forehead furrowed.

He pressed the stop button on the recorder and said, "Excuse me for just a moment," before exiting the room.

Vertice turned her attention to a fly stuck in the overhead lighting. It was buzzing frantically and repeatedly flying into the plastic covering, making a light knocking sound. She wondered why it didn't stop.

# CHAPTER TWELVE

The first night Anna and Cayden spent together was filled with laughter. They played five games of Candy Land, colored in Cayden's Batman coloring book, made Jello Jigglers and watched the movie *Casper* on television. Finally Cayden fell asleep curled up in Anna's lap. Rather than disturb him, she sat there watching him sleep until dozing off herself around three o'clock in the morning. She was completely in love with him, more so even than when she gave birth to him, more so than with any person who had ever been in her life. She was surprised by just how instantaneous the feeling was.

Anna awoke thinking Ginger was climbing all over her trying to wake her for a walk. In fact, it was Cayden.

"Wake up, Mommy!" he was saying while pulling on her limbs. Anna thought that she would never tire of hearing herself called that. He pulled her left sock off and tickled her toes.

"Stop that, you little monster!" She grabbed him, throwing his body down on the couch cushion and tickling his tummy, loving the sound of his hysterical laughter.

Anna watched Ginger look up sheepishly from her spot on the rug, seemingly jealous of all of the attention and affection the new little boy was receiving.

"Let's put our shoes on," Anna said, "and take Ginger for a walk. Whaddya say?"

Cayden leaped off the couch, pretending he was a plane, and made engine noises while he located his sneakers.

He carried them over to Anna and climbed into her lap.

"Do you know how to tie your shoes?"

He shook his head.

"First we take each string in one hand." She wrapped his tiny fingers around one of the laces and then did the same with the other lace. "And then we make a loop with both ends, and pull them through each other to form a knot." She guided his hands to finish the bow. "Excellent, Einstein!" She ruffled his thick wavy hair with her fingers. "You must have very intelligent genes!" He smiled broadly, obviously proud of himself. "Now let's do the other."

After the walk with Ginger, during which Cayden insisted on holding the leash, they returned to the apartment for breakfast. Anna didn't have any cereal since her traditional breakfast consisted of four cups of coffee. "How about some toast and jam?" she asked.

He shook his head no.

Of course not, what kid would want boring toast? Peering into the refrigerator, she offered, "Scrambled eggs with melted cheese?"

He scrunched up his nose. "Yuck! Baby chickens!"

She made a mental note about the eggs. "Cottage cheese?"

He made gagging sounds. "Eww!"

"Okay, Mr. Picky, tell me what you usually have."

"Daddy makes pancakes on Saturdays."

"Oh, well, Mommy can make pancakes too." Anna found a box of Bisquick in the cupboard. As she prepared the batter, with his help mixing, of course, she asked, "Have you ever had Mickey Mouse pancakes?"

"No," he answered, wiping batter off his arm and looking up at her excitedly.

"Well, I am the Mickey Mouse pancake queen!"

"Teach me!" he shouted while jumping up to try to see above the island.

"Come here, jumping bean." She scooped him up in her arms and hugged him.

He rubbed his nose against hers. "Eskimo kisses!"

* * *

Anna had to meet with Connors twice more to discuss the details of Ian's trust and to handle the legal matters related to taking over guardianship of Cayden. She would miss some classes, including Lexy's, but, with Cayden, she probably wouldn't be able to finish the semester anyway.

She was surprised to find that she was the primary beneficiary of Ian's life insurance policy as well as the trustee of his rather large estate, which included much of the settlement he had received from Christian's wrongful death case. Her initial fears about being able to care for Cayden monetarily were quickly dispelled by Ian's attorney.

Nevertheless, for the time being, she decided Cayden would sleep with her in her queen-sized bed. He'd had enough changes lately and was relatively content with his new living arrangement, especially because of Ginger, who was very patient as Cayden tugged on her ears and tail and tried to ride her like a horse. Anna knew, however, that she'd eventually need to look into getting a larger place for the two of them so Cayden could have a room of his own. She remembered how hard it was for Ian to get Cayden to sleep in his own bedroom. He had complained to her about it on the phone.

By Wednesday, Anna had quit her job at the bar and decided to withdraw from all of her classes. She wouldn't have the time for any of that now, it was clear. She felt that she owed Lexy an explanation for having stormed out of class the previous week though. If she left things the way they were, Lexy would likely think that Anna had withdrawn because of her.

She'd go see her in person, she decided, maybe even introduce her to Cayden. She was nervous, however, about how she would react to the new love of her life, the little boy whom she had just taught to tie his shoes.

\* \* \*

Jennifer was shocked to find a police cruiser idling outside her home when she returned from school on Thursday afternoon. The two uniformed officers asked her if she would come with them to the station for questioning.

"What about?"

"Ma'am, please don't misunderstand," one of the officers said. "You are not being taken into custody, nor are you under suspicion of anything. We'd simply like to ask you a few questions in the hopes that you may have helpful information pertaining to a murder investigation."

"*Murder?*"

\* \* \*

It had been more than a week since the T.S. Eliot lecture and Anna had not returned to class. When Lexy received the automated notice from the registrar alerting her to Anna's withdrawal, she was overcome with guilt. Their association had clearly damaged Anna's academics. That was what she had been trying to avoid. She'd thought about dropping by Anna's place to apologize or visiting the bar to talk with her, but she decided that it was probably better to let things alone. She'd only further complicate things.

At the Community Center that evening, Lexy had tried desperately to keep her mind fixed on the live model, but thoughts of Anna continued to creep in. Every figure she had sculpted for weeks looked like her. Every figure, no matter the position or the model's features, was another Anna.

*My life is perfectly fine. It was perfectly fine before Anna and will be perfectly fine after her too,* she told herself when she got home. *Well, except for having sixty papers to grade by Monday.*

She was sitting on her sofa, writing a note in the margin of a student paper and half-listening to the ten o'clock news, when she heard the newscaster ask, "Is an obsessed fan perpetrating murders that mirror those in the works of Florida author J. Deveaux?"

Her head snapped up at the mention of Jennifer's pen name. "That's one of the theories of local law enforcement following the September fifth death of Samantha Jensen..." The camera zoomed in on a sheet-draped body "...found mutilated in the Key West apartment she shared with her fiancé. The particulars of this murder and murders in York, Maine, and Portsmouth, New Hampshire, mirror details in J. Deveaux's three thriller-suspense novels..."

Lexy stared open-mouthed as an image of Jennifer's books fanned out like a poker hand on the screen. *Oh my god!* She reached for her cell phone.

\* \* \*

Reilly received an email response from the Key West PD reporting that Ari Flemming's alibi had been confirmed by a Bradley Whittaker, who had "complied fully" and answered all questions without an attorney present. He also learned that Jennifer Gardiner had been located by the OCPD and was cooperating with the investigation.

He pressed the preset speed dial button on his office phone.

"Cole here," the gruff voice answered.

"Jennifer's been brought in."

"In custody?" Agent Cole's speech, normally hard, blunt and steady, was now, Reilly noticed, higher-pitched and sounding slightly panicked.

"No, she's volunteered to answer questions."

"Do they have anything on her?"

"Not yet."

* * *

Jennifer wiped at her eyes, the tears unrelenting. She'd already heard about the murder and the connection to her books on the news, but she couldn't help but be overwhelmed with emotion as the detective confirmed Mona, Teresa and Samantha's passings.

"You understand, Dr. Gardiner, that the questions I'm about to ask you are routine, and in no way should indicate that we suspect your involvement in Samantha Jensen's murder. You are not in our custody and are answering these questions voluntarily, which means that you are welcome to leave at any time. You're also welcome to have an attorney present."

She waved her hand in the air dismissively.

"I need you to express understanding vocally...for the record."

"I understand," she muttered.

"Jennifer." That was the first time Detective Parker had used such a familiar address in their conversation. It made her uncomfortable. "Do you remember where you were on Saturday, September fifth, specifically between the hours of three and four p.m.?"

"I...I was staying in a friend's cottage in Marathon in the Keys."

"We'll need that friend's name so that he or she can corroborate your whereabouts."

"Her name's Star Brandenberg."

"How do you know this Ms. Brandenberg?"

"We had a fling at a writer's retreat a while back and have been friends ever since. I don't see her often because she travels a lot. She's a novelist. Pretty famous. Maybe you've heard of her?" The detective shook his head. "Anyway, she has a cottage near a fish camp in Marathon. I keep an eye on the place, visiting every other month or so while Star's traveling to research story settings—make sure the plumbing and air are working. It's not much, but it's quiet and I needed to get away."

"Why did you need to get away?"

"I had a lot of...stuff going on here. Lexy, my closest friend, and I had gotten into a fight. I was having business issues with my publisher, who turned out to not even be my publisher at all! And I was getting the cold shoulder right and left from a woman I was interested in."

"How can we contact this Ms. Brandenberg?"

"I have an address and cell phone number in my contact list." She fished her cell phone out of her pocket.

"So, between the hours of three and four?"

"I don't know. I was either in the cottage or on the beach."

"Were you with anyone? Did anyone see you?"

"Maybe someone saw me. I wasn't feeling very social, though, so I didn't do much. I did go down to Frank's Crab Shack to have a beer. I don't know when that was though. Sometime on Saturday." Jennifer began searching through the front pocket of the canvas shoulder bag she had brought with her. "I still have the key to the cottage," she said, holding up a brass key on a plastic pineapple keychain.

After a beat, the detective said, "We'd like to search the cottage and your residence, Dr. Gardiner. We'll contact this Ms. Brandenberg about the cottage, but we'd like your permission to search your home." Jennifer, unsure of how to respond, sat blinking at the detective. He pushed the box of tissues in her direction. "We'd prefer to not have to secure a warrant," he said.

"You don't think I have something to do with this, do you?" She tried to hide the trembling of her voice. "You don't think I'm involved?"

"I certainly don't mean to be implying that, Dr. Gardiner." Detective Parker smiled. "We'd simply like your voluntary cooperation in this investigation."

"Yes, fine," she muttered, dabbing at her eyes. "Search my house."

\* \* \*

"Hello?"

"Lex, it's me." Jennifer sounded flustered. "The police are searching my house!"

"What?" Lexy remembered the image of the sheet-draped body being carried from the apartment.

"Why are they searching *your* house?"

"They asked, and I don't have anything to hide." Lexy could hear Jennifer cover up the mouthpiece with her palm. "Can you please be careful with that? It's Sonoma!" she said.

"Oh my god!" Lexy grabbed her Windbreaker off the closet hanger. "I'm coming over."

"No, it's okay. If I need support, I'll call Andy..." Lexy heard something fall. "Jeez, I said be careful!" Jennifer shouted.

"*Andy*? Why her?"

"We've been...It's a long story. Don't touch that vase! Listen, Lex, I've gotta go. I'll be fine."

"Jennifer, wait—"

The phone went dead.

# CHAPTER THIRTEEN

Lexy had left seven voice mail messages for Jennifer since she'd hung up with her the night before but had yet to receive a return call. By now, she decided, Jennifer had undoubtedly heard of Samantha's passing and the suspicion that a deranged reader was reconstructing the fictional murders in her books— she imagined Jennifer had to be consumed with guilt.

*And who does she turn to for support?* Not her friend of three years—the friend who spent hours on the phone with her after Samantha took up with that guy, the friend who listened to her go on and on about this or that new love interest. No, turning to a friend whom she could trust would make too much sense for Jennifer. Instead, she turns to the four-monther whose pants she wants to get into. Or is in already.

Lexy retreated to her office and tried to focus on her grading, but she was only going through the motions. Her mind was completely preoccupied with Jennifer and with Samantha. She couldn't believe she was gone! They'd met at the luncheon for the incoming tenure-track class. Samantha was Jennifer's "plus one." With her well-groomed arching brows, high cheekbones and perfectly coiffed Jennifer Aniston 'do, she looked like a model. She didn't quite have the carriage, height or allure of a Victoria's Secret model but she was definitely attractive—Loft catalog quality, Lexy thought. They seemed happy together—Jennifer and Samantha—sampling each other's meals and laughing over intimate jokes.

Samantha had been the first of Jennifer's dates that Lexy could imagine sticking around for more than the post-sex shower. And she did—she moved in, in fact. And life had continued in storybook fashion until the cheating. "She's a slut! A whore!" The language, the rage in Jennifer's voice had shocked Lexy. Jennifer had been flirting with other women all along and Lexy had assumed that she and Samantha had some sort of understanding. Apparently, they didn't.

Lexy breathed a sigh of relief when she heard the knock at her office door, thinking that it must be Jennifer. She minimized the Excel spreadsheet of grades on the computer and turned to the door.

It wasn't Jennifer though. It was Anna. She could see her through the door's vertical window, the bottom half of which was covered by editorial cartoons, blocking her view of anything below her shoulders. Anna's eyes were facing downward. Was she nervous or embarrassed or too angry to look her in the eye? Lexy swallowed hard as Anna's words echoed in her memory: "That's not what you meant at all, is it, Dr. Strayer?" She was right of course. She hadn't meant it. She hadn't meant to lead her on. She hadn't meant to hurt her. And she hadn't meant to feel for her what she had, what she still was feeling.

When she opened the door, she discovered to her surprise that Anna wasn't alone. Swinging from her arm, as if it were a Tarzan vine, was an adorable little boy.

"Hi," Anna said.

"Hi." Lexy was temporarily stunned by the resemblance between Anna and the boy. The same thick dark hair. The same deep green eyes. The same long lashes. A brother?

"May we come in?" Anna had never come to her office before and Lexy felt somehow unprotected. She was thankful to have the desk to hide behind.

"Of course," she said.

Anna sat in one of the two chairs that faced Lexy's desk. The boy stretched his arms out to her. "Up!" he said, smiling at her. "Please?" Anna lifted him, and he settled comfortably in her lap. He was holding a stuffed toy—a dinosaur or a dragon, Lexy wasn't sure.

"This is Cayden." Cayden looked up when he heard his name and put his hands over his face bashfully. "Cayden, meet Professor Strayer." The boy opened his hands as if he were playing peek-a-boo and shot Lexy a big toothy grin.

"Hi, Cayden," Lexy said, not sure if she should wave at him or shake his hand.

Cayden buried his face in Anna's sweatshirt. "He's a little shy," she said.

Lexy took in the two of them, thinking it was the cutest picture she'd ever seen. She wished she could have a snapshot of this moment.

"I'm sorry about class...my little breakdown...and I'm sorry about the opera." Anna wet her finger and wiped at Cayden's cheek where there was a spot of what looked to be dried syrup.

"*I'm* sorry. I shouldn't have..." Her eyes fell on the boy. "I think I might have sent mixed signals." Lexy watched Cayden pull the zipper of Anna's sweatshirt up and down. "Your brother is absolutely adorable!" Lexy said. "You two have the same eyes."

Anna bit her lower lip. Cayden, having grown bored with the zipper, was trying to get down. Anna repositioned him so that he was facing Lexy. "He's not my brother."

Lexy suddenly wanted to close the office door, but she remained seated. She folded her arms across her chest and looked away from them at a nail hole in the far wall where a painting once hung. Her eye twitched.

"Cayden is my son."

"Your *son*?" Lexy felt light-headed. She put her hands flat on the desk so as to keep herself from falling.

Anna covered Cayden's ears with her hands. "His father…" She didn't complete her sentence. Cayden was pulling at her fingers and growing frustrated. "Well, maybe I'll explain another day," she said as she released her hold on the boy.

"Mommy, when are we going to ride the duck?"

"Soon, sweetie," she answered. "He means the swan paddle-boats at the lake."

"Nice." Lexy was still stunned.

"I withdrew from all of my classes when C-A-Y-D-E-N and his father's lawyer showed up on my doorstep. I'm sure you can understand."

"Of course." Truthfully, she didn't, but this clearly wasn't the time to go into it.

Anna picked up Cayden and deposited him on the carpet. She took his hand. "Well, we're off to ride some swans."

As Lexy watched them go, she remembered the many conversations she and Jules had had about having children. The memory of the last one brought tears to her eyes.

Jules's temperature often fluctuated during the chemotherapy sessions, but on that particular day, she had been so chilled that her teeth chattered. Lexy rubbed her arms to warm her.

"Lex," she had said, "I don't think I can do this much longer."

Lexy tried to stay strong for Jules, but it was no use. The tears came instantly. "I can't lose you." She rested her head in her lover's lap. "You're my everything."

"I'm not your everything. You'll go on. You'll have a full and wonderful life."

Lexy just cried into the wool blanket that was wrapped around Jules's middle, unable to speak.

"You'll meet some gorgeous woman and have beautiful babies together."

The thought that the children she and Jules had been planning to have would never be, made her cry more violently.

In that moment, Lexy realized that she didn't want Anna and Cayden to go. She could hear them making their way down the hallway. "Anna?" she called after them.

"Yeah?"

"Do you want some company? Those swans are pretty hard for one person to pedal."

\* \* \*

Anna had Cayden on her shoulders. He was giggling as she stood up on her toes so that he could reach the high branch where they had just spotted a squirrel. The squirrel was long gone, of course, but Cayden wanted to see for himself. Lexy was left holding his blue Smurf-flavored ice cream cone, which was dripping down her hand in the hot sun.

"Hurry up, little man, or your ice cream is going to be nothing more than a puddle when you come back."

Cayden turned, his face filled with concern. "Mommy…"

Anna trotted him over to where Lexy was standing and crouched down slightly so Lexy could pass him his sugar cone.

"Don't drip that Smurf stuff on my hair," Anna said just as a blue drip splattered onto her cheek.

Lexy reached over and caught the drop with her index finger. Their eyes met as they had so many times before. Anna wet her lips in response.

After sufficiently cleaning off Anna's cheek, Lexy placed her finger in her own mouth. "So that's what Smurfs taste like," she said, laughing.

"Yeah, repulsive thought, right? I used to like Smurfs. Well, Smurfette, anyway," Anna chirped. "Maybe we'll finish our ice cream on Mother Earth instead of on Mommy." She pried Cayden's body from her shoulders and placed him carefully on the grass. He immediately sat down Indian style and licked at his ice cream, which was now all over his face and hands.

Lexy and Anna sat down too.

"So, what do you think about all this?" Lexy asked.

"I'm happy." Anna did look happy, Lexy thought. "I think my purpose in life has found me instead of the other way around." She laughed as Cayden dripped ice cream onto his red Nike T-shirt. "I love him so much that love doesn't even seem to cover it."

Lexy smiled.

"His father was my best friend, and he and his partner wanted a baby. Florida law didn't allow for gay adoption at the time," she said. "So, Ian and I had Cayden."

"What happened to Ian?"

Even though Cayden didn't appear to be listening, Anna answered, "He went to heaven."

"So, Cayden's yours—for good?"

"Yup. I'm an instant mommy." She smiled as Cayden climbed into her lap, leaving a sticky blue mess everywhere he touched.

"The mommy thing agrees with you." Lexy squeezed Anna's shoulder.

"Thanks."

"I mean it. You look…" She studied the other woman. "You look more alive than you ever have before. Happier. You're sort of glowing."

"Yeah, but can I still look…*lovely*…even when I'm covered in blue goo?"

Lexy remembered the opera and Anna in her strapless gown. Her stomach fluttered nervously at the memory of Anna's voice saying, "I want to kiss you."

"You look lovely right now," she said.

Anna blushed.

"And you, sir, are very handsome." Lexy tousled Cayden's hair and he scrunched up his face in response. "It must run in the family."

* * *

Lexy had so much fun with Anna and Cayden at SeaWorld on Saturday that she almost forgot about Jennifer and the newscast. On the drive home, Cayden excitedly retold the story of the show they'd seen with Clyde the sea lion and Seamore the otter—several times. Despite his excitement, or perhaps because of it, he was fast asleep by the time they made it to Anna's apartment, curled up in the backseat with the new stuffed Shamu doll that Lexy had bought for him.

"I think he's out for days," Anna said, picking him up in her arms. She struggled to balance his weight so that she could free one hand to unlock the door. "Lexy, do you think you could help us?"

Lexy took the keys, which were dangling from her fingers under Cayden's body, and let them in.

Anna went to tuck him in, while Lexy, unsure if she should leave or stay, stood awkwardly in the center of the living room, tossing the keys from one hand to the other.

"I think we've exhausted the poor thing." Anna came around the corner and, upon finding Lexy still there, smiled.

"Yeah, I'm sure you're pretty tired out too. Maybe we could do something later in the week though—like go to the movies together or something." Lexy felt like a teenager and stared at her shoes.

"Actually, I'm not ready for bed yet. Want to join me for a glass of wine?"

"I'd love to."

Anna motioned Lexy to sit down on the sofa and disappeared into the kitchen. She returned with two balloon-shaped wineglasses and an opened bottle of pinot noir. "I hope this is okay," she said, raising the bottle slightly. "It was already open."

"That's fine." Lexy was incredibly nervous. She wasn't sure why.

"Cheers." Anna clinked her glass into Lexy's.

"To the new addition in your life."

"Yes, the new addition." They sipped their wine. Anna relaxed, pressing her head and shoulders into the back of the sofa, and sighed. "I'm so content right now."

"Yeah?"

"Yeah, I don't think I've ever felt like this before. Nothing's bothering me, just a peaceful calm." Anna closed her eyes, smiling.

"You look peaceful," Lexy said, studying Anna's face as the muscles around her eyes and lips relaxed. She wanted to touch her face, to feel its softness, to run her hands through the woman's thick mane. She wanted to press her lips to the quiet pulsing she saw in Anna's neck. She watched her breathe, the slow rise and fall of her chest. She leaned toward her, her body seeming to move of its own accord. She breathed in her scent, reminiscent of blackberries and sage. And she couldn't help but move closer.

Lexy hovered above Anna's resting form, remembering the image of her with her son on her shoulders at the park, a splotch of blue ice cream on her cheek, and she felt something break inside her. She was afraid she would cry. She recognized this feeling. She had felt it once before. With Jules.

She hated what thoughts of Jules brought with them—the tubes, one connected to her nose to help with her breathing and one in her arm for the intravenous feed, the wires that seemed to pour out of her hospital gown, and the machines that surrounded the bed and blinked numbers and lights that Lexy didn't understand. It was close to the end...six days before Jules disappeared forever. The bit of sky that Lexy could see through the slits in the hospital blinds was gray and flat, just like she felt. "Don't let yourself waste away," Jules had said, reaching for Lexy's hand. Her voice sounded harsh and Lexy was sure it pained her to talk. "I know you, Lexy Strayer; you'd rather let life happen to you than direct it." She coughed and struggled to catch her breath. "I want you to direct it."

"Anna," Lexy breathed, her eyes fixed on the woman's lips. Anna's green eyes fluttered open.

Lexy brushed the side of her face softly with her hand and moved closer, wetting her lips with her tongue... And then their lips found each other.

Lexy was struck first by the softness that greeted her. Anna opened to her, inviting her in, her arms wrapping around Lexy's body, pulling her closer, her tongue seductively sliding into her mouth.

Lexy had never been so turned on by just a kiss. Her body was pulsing with desire. She felt as though she'd lost her connection to the world. All of her attention, every nerve ending in her body had come alive and was now focused on this kiss, this woman.

She could feel Anna's fingers pluck at the buttons on her blouse. And then her hand stilled and her lips broke away.

"What is it?"

"We can't do this now...not with Cayden in the house," Anna said, her breathing labored and hoarse. "He could wake up."

"You're right," Lexy managed, struggling to button her blouse back up. She turned away from Anna and prepared to rise from the sofa and move toward the door.

Anna pulled Lexy's chin toward her so that their eyes were aligned. "I don't *want* to stop, Lexy," she said.

"I understand." Lexy finished buttoning her blouse. "I should go." She felt empty somehow, as though she were missing something. She silently catalogued her belongings: keys, cell, wallet...

The two women walked to the door.

"Thank you...for today."

Anna smiled and kissed Lexy softly on the lips. "Don't you run away now, Beautiful. We're just getting started," she whispered into her ear.

Those words played over and over again in Lexy's mind as she drove home.

* * *

Star Brandenberg was sitting outdoors at a little café in Paris sipping her *café au lait* and picking at her croissant Sunday afternoon when her Prada purse came alive with the sprightly notes of Vivaldi's "Four Seasons." She reached into it to quiet her cell phone.

"Hello?"

"Ms. Brandenberg?"

"Yes?"

Star removed her large Prada sunglasses, specifically chosen to match her purse, and set them on the table.

"I'm Detective Parker from the Orange County Police Department."

Star sat up straighter, feeling the iron chair backing pressing on her shoulders. "Detective, what can I do for you?"

"If you have a few moments, I'd like to ask you some questions pertaining to a friend of yours, Jennifer Gardiner."

Hearing the familiar name sent a shiver of fear up her spine. "Jennifer? Is she okay?"

"She's fine, Ms. Brandenberg. Dr. Gardiner told us that she was staying in your cottage in Marathon, Florida, over the Labor Day weekend. Is that correct?"

"Yes. Jennifer stays there quite often. In fact, she's a godsend! I don't know what I'd do if I didn't have a friend in the States to check in on the place." *Did I overdo it?* she wondered. "Is she in some kind of trouble?"

"Do you know for a fact that she was there on Saturday, September fifth?"

"Well, I'm sure if she says she was there, she was there."

"Did you speak with Dr. Gardiner over that weekend?"

"I think I talked to her late Friday evening."

"But you're not sure?"

"No, I mean, I'm sure I talked to her. I'm just not sure if it was Friday or Saturday. Listen, can you tell me what this is about?"

"Are you familiar with Dr. Gardiner's novels?"

"Of course."

"Well, three of the murders in her books have been replicated."

"Meaning?"

"Meaning that three women are dead, Ms. Brandenberg, and we're trying to get to the bottom of it."

"Well, certainly you don't think that Jennifer has anything to do with that!"

"We're trying to rule that out."

After hanging up, Star massaged the tight muscles in her neck. *How long am I going to have to put up with this?* she wondered. *How much longer can I fight my conscience?*

* * *

On Monday evening, Lexy took Anna and Cayden to a local playhouse that performed puppet shows and other children's theater.

Heavy maroon curtains, held by braided gold ropes, framed the little puppet stage. The puppets themselves had exaggerated features: long, almost-Pinocchio noses and extremely high cheekbones. They wore colorful costumes and their faces were painted in clownish makeup. The hair on some was painted on, while others had crazy Afros and pigtails made from yarn. Cayden clapped excitedly when the mustached villain was clobbered by a piano that dropped from the sky.

Lexy studied Anna, who sat on the carpeted floor with the other parents, Cayden in her lap, gasping and clapping along with him at all the right times. She couldn't help but think of all the venues to which she might have taken Anna before: romantic restaurants, the theater, even dancing. She regretted not having done those things when she had had the chance. Why hadn't they ever danced together or tasted each other's entrees over a candlelit dinner for two? She remembered the opera. Their only date, Lexy thought now.

She couldn't remember any longer why it had seemed so important to push Anna away. If she could return now to that night in Anna's apartment, the evening would have ended much differently. She regretted not having responded to Anna's overtures. And she regretted not having pursued her with the fervor and passion that she certainly felt.

Just then, Anna began winding Cayden's dark wavy hair around her fingers, which brought Lexy back to the first day of class. Anna had been sitting in what would become her usual seat, and as Lexy read from the syllabus, she had seen Anna wind her wavy hair around her fingers, just as she was doing now with Cayden's locks. She had seen her do that many times since they'd met. It was something Lexy had come to find incredibly endearing about her. And as she watched Anna coil Cayden's curls around her finger in the same manner she had seen her do so many times with her own hair, Lexy suddenly felt what she imagined writers meant when they described a squeezing in a character's chest, a pain in her heart. Anna was smiling, her eyes on Cayden, rather than the stage, and Lexy imagined them as a family. The thought made her feel complete, in a way she had never felt before. *This* moment she wouldn't trade for any romantic dinner or theater show. Theirs was no fairy tale, no polished romance. But this moment at the puppet show, watching the woman she loved play with her son's hair, was all that she needed—all that she'd ever need.

\* \* \*

Cocktail sauce had spilled onto Rita Phillips's left hand from the fried shrimp basket she had just delivered to the young man at the end of the bar. After wiping her hand off on her apron, she returned to filling the mug with beer from the tap. The damn thing needed to be fixed. Always sputtering and jerking, occasionally spraying the bar with foam. Thank god it hadn't yet soaked a customer, she thought to herself.

It being a Tuesday night, Frank's Crab Shack was pretty empty. Only a few of the regular crowd clung to their mugs, staring into the foam head as if it held the answers to life. Even the pool table remained silent, absent the usual sounds made by sticks striking balls or balls clanking through the maze of inner piping. The only chairs that were filled in the entire place were those at the bar.

"How 'bout one on the house, Rita...for your best customer?" The slurred words served as evidence of how much alcohol the speaker had already consumed.

Rita leaned over the counter, purposely resting her large breasts on the railing. "Nothin's for free, Todd, you know that."

Todd, a twenty-something guy with a clean-shaven boyish face, was currently staring at Rita's low-cut neckline through his sleepy-looking eyes, and smoking a cigarette.

"Don't you fall under that whore's spell!" bellowed the balding man dressed in a cheap blue suit seated next to him. He slapped Todd playfully on the shoulder. "She ain't that good in bed!"

Rita scowled at the older man and began cleaning off the bar with a wet rag.

"You should mind your manners, old man...This here's a *lady*." Each word melted into the next. Todd looked sheepishly at his empty glass and then up at Rita.

"Flatter me all you like, Stevens. But business is business!"

Just then Rita noticed a man, better dressed than most of the customers that frequented Frank's Crab Shack, enter the restaurant through the side entrance. Rita's eyes fell on his shiny loafers. The man made his way to the bar, eyeing Todd Sullivan and the older man suspiciously.

"Ma'am?" he said when he reached Rita.

She smiled.

He flipped open a leather case, revealing a silver badge. "I'm Detective Dobbs with the Key West Police Department. Is the owner or manager present?" he asked.

Rita shook her head. "Just little ole me tonight."

"Well, I wonder if I could ask you a few questions, Missus..."

Rita took in the detective's impressively muscular form. "It's Phillips, and it's Miss," she said, batting her eyelashes at him.

"Were you working on the afternoon of September fifth? That was a Saturday."

Todd Sullivan, overhearing the conversation, nudged the older man next to him with his elbow. "Someone's in trouble," he said.

"I work every Saturday, Detective." Rita wiped at the counter in front of Detective Dobbs with her rag.

"Well, I wonder if you can tell me if you recall a particular woman coming in for a beer on that Saturday."

The detective pulled a photograph out of the pocket of the dark green folder he was holding and held it out for Rita to see.

She studied the woman's short reddish-brown hair and light blue eyes. "Yeah, I remember her. But she didn't get just a beer." She laughed.

"What do you mean?"

"She had maybe three beers and a couple tequila shots that Saturday. I remember because she made a little scene before she left."

"What kind of scene?"

"Well, she was pretty sloshed, and she was hittin' on one of my customer's girlfriends. We don't get that much here."

"Oh, I see." Detective Dobbs jotted a note down on a spiral notepad. "Do you recall what time the woman left the restaurant?"

"Yeah, it was just before my lunch break. I'd say around one thirty." Again, the detective wrote something down.

"Hey, copper!" barked the guy in the blue suit, causing Detective Dobbs to turn in his direction. "Yer lookin' for that Jennifer, aren't ya?"

"Do you know Jennifer Gardiner?"

"Yeah. She comes in here all snooty, thinking she's better than everybody else…She called me a Neanderthal. *Bitch*. And she hit on Jimbo's little woman."

"Don't mind the alkie, Detective," Rita said, tossing a quick but judgmental look at the man, as if to corroborate the Neanderthal characterization. "He's just pissed that your redhead turned him down. He can barely remember how he got here, let alone what happened on a certain day in September."

Detective Dobbs seemed to take in the man's cheap suit and then turned back to Rita. After jotting down her name and contact information, he said, "Thanks so much for your time, ma'am."

"Anytime, Detective," Rita answered, wishing she were close enough to run her hands over those impressive biceps of his.

# CHAPTER FOURTEEN

Lexy received a frantic call from Jennifer Tuesday evening; she was crying so much that she was almost utterly incoherent. Lexy couldn't make sense of all that she was saying except that the police search of her house had apparently unearthed something and they had called her into the police station for more questioning.

She had hated to leave Anna and Cayden, having just settled in with a big bowl of popcorn to watch a Pixar movie in Anna's living room, but her friend needed her.

Lexy drove at least twenty miles over the speed limit the entire way to the Orange County police station.

The plump redhead in the traditional blue police uniform at the front desk was on the phone. Lexy stood impatiently waiting for her to hang up.

"Yeah, well, you don't take a woman to a county fair if you're trying to impress her!" she was saying into the phone. "I mean, he promised me dinner. And a cheesesteak ain't what I had in mind!"

Lexy stood there for several minutes until she could stand waiting no longer. The woman was obviously having some sort of personal conversation. "Excuse me?" she said, unable to hide the irritation in her voice.

The redhead snorted into the phone, peering at Lexy out of the corner of her eye. "Hang on a minute, Sheila." She set the phone down on the counter and turned to Lexy, chewing her gum with her mouth open. "Yes?" the woman asked while fluffing the side of her unnaturally red curly hair and opening a compact mirror. Lexy hated this woman.

"My friend Jennifer Gardiner has been taken in for questioning!" Lexy's nerves were on edge, and although she knew her voice was panicked and a bit too loud, she didn't care.

"You aren't allowed back. You'll have to wait for your friend over there." She motioned to the plastic yellow and green seats that lined the waiting room area. Her fake smile revealed lipstick-smeared teeth.

"No, *you* don't understand. She called me! My name's Lexy Strayer. She must've left my name with you." Lexy glanced at the ledger-like book open on the desk in front of the redhead.

"Like I said." The woman's expression was stony, her lips slightly pursed. "You can wait in the waiting area like everybody else."

Lexy, thinking she finally understood what feeling emasculated truly meant, walked toward the seating area. She heard the woman pick up the conversation where she had left off.

"So I says to him, where's the romance..."

Lexy sat down across from a middle-aged couple. The woman was sobbing, and the bearded, bespectacled man was consoling her. Lexy decided that they must be there because of a teenager who had gotten arrested for drunk and disorderly conduct or pulling some sort of fraternity prank. She wondered what Cayden would be like at that age.

"It's okay, Helen," the man was saying. "Tom said with first-offense misdemeanors like this, they usually get a fine."

"But it's Jeffrey, not somebody else's kid, Hank. It's Jeffrey," the woman said between sobs.

What would it be like, Lexy wondered, to have a son? What would it feel like to worry about him when he forgot to take his lunch money to school, when he went on his first date, when he didn't come home by his curfew? She imagined a grown-up Cayden, handsome and tall, his hair unruly, thick and dark like his mother's. She imagined him in a graduation cap and gown and she and Anna in the audience smiling proudly when his name was announced. She wondered if he'd be straight and bring young girls home to meet his mother or if he'd be gay and worry that he wouldn't be accepted by his schoolmates. She wondered if he'd like sports, playing an instrument—maybe the saxophone or the drums, or if he'd be an artist—a painter or a sculptor. She imagined Christmases and holidays, sparklers on Independence Day and pool party barbecues with friends in the backyard. She imagined bringing him to gay pride marches and little Cayden waving a rainbow flag on a stick.

"What kind of parents are we? How could we not have known?" the woman asked.

Then Lexy imagined a teenaged Cayden—his hair dyed blue and on his feet big leather boots closed with buckles and metal clasps—being rebellious and arguing with his mother. She imagined sitting across from a teacher speaking disapprovingly of Cayden at a parent-teacher conference. She imagined being here at the police station, waiting in this yellow plastic seat and worrying about what was going to happen to him. She could almost feel the nervousness in her stomach, the fear pulsing through her veins, the disappointment in her heart, but still she imagined that there was love overshadowing everything else. Unconditional love. She could see it unmistakably stamped on the woman's face.

\* \* \*

Adalia Johnson, having already struck a deal with the Key West PD that pinned the majority of charges related to their gunrunning business on JoJo, her boyfriend, had been answering Detective Bunson's questions for almost forty minutes now.

"Is this almost over? I'm starving!"

Detective Bunson eyed the woman's fatty forearms and frowned. "Yes, soon...So, you say that a dark-haired woman, seeming confused, came into the lobby a little after three p.m.?"

"Yeah, she seemed really out of it, like maybe she was on something, only she didn't really look the type. She just sort of pushed this paper at me and asked if I could help her. I figured she was just trying to track her friend down or something." Adalia noticed some crumbs in the detective's mustache.

Bunson, as if reading her mind, wiped his hand over his upper lip. "What *was* on the paper, Ms. Johnson?"

"Sam and John's names and the Blue Parrot's address." Adalia yawned, revealing a number of metal fillings.

"In what way did she seem confused?" Bunson fingered what looked to be a pack of cigarettes in his pocket.

"Well, she was all looking around at stuff like she was tryin' to figger out where the hell she wuz."

"And what did you tell her?"

"I gave her John's apartment number."

"Would you be willing to go through a few photos to see if you can identify the woman?"

"I'd rather go home and eat!" Adalia's stomach rumbled on cue.

"It shouldn't take long," he said as he pulled a blue plastic lighter out of his pocket and began to turn it over in his hand.

"Fine!" Adalia said irritably.

* * *

Jennifer's lawyer, who had up until that moment only looked over her condo lease agreement and her royalty contracts with Flemming Press, felt completely out of place in the chilly investigation room. He had spent his career looking over documents, mortgage agreements, estate trusts and wills; he'd never had a client accused of murder.

Jennifer, seemingly beside herself with confusion and sadness, was dabbing at her mascara-smeared eyes with a balled-up tissue.

"Dr. Gardiner, Detective Dobbs with the Key West PD was able to confirm that you were seen at Frank's Crab Shack in Marathon on Saturday, September fifth, by a waitress and a customer. However, the waitress reported that you left the restaurant at half past one. Marathon is approximately a one-hour drive from Key West, where the murder took place. Is there anyone who can verify your whereabouts between one thirty and four p.m.?"

"No, but I was probably on the beach or in the cottage."

"We also had a question about something we found in your residence: a receipt from a 7-Eleven in Key West. The receipt places you in the area at two twenty-seven p.m. on that Saturday."

The receipt the detective showed them was for Winterfresh Gum and bottled water, purchased with cash. It could have been anyone's; it certainly wasn't enough to link Jennifer to the crime scene.

"Where did they find the receipt?"

"In a drawer. I don't see how that—"

"My girlfriend was in Key West over Labor Day weekend. Maybe it was hers."

The detective ruffled through some papers. "And you weren't with her?"

"As I said earlier, we were having some problems." Jennifer looked down as if embarrassed.

"Who's your girlfriend?"

"Andy."

"And she is?"

"She teaches English at OCC. Andy Cole."

"Andy Cole?" he spluttered, almost choking on his water. Jennifer nodded. "*She's* your girlfriend?"

# CHAPTER FIFTEEN

"I cannot believe that you would jeopardize this case by having relations with the suspect!" The purple vein in Assistant Director William Benton's forehead was swollen and pulsing.

Andy sat staring at her badge, which he had asked her to surrender only moments before.

"If Internal Affairs didn't need you alive, I would strangle you!" he said, his voice filled with disgust. "My god, Cole, what the hell were you thinking?"

She didn't answer him, fighting back tears, but just sat staring at her silver badge on his desk, which glinted in the sunlight that shone through the plate glass window on the far wall.

She was thinking of her partner, Seth, and the day of the second annual Police/Fire Softball Tournament. It had been maybe ninety-eight degrees that day and humid as hell. Her jersey was wet with perspiration before they had even begun playing. Seth and Andy were sitting in the dugout waiting to bat when he had suddenly turned to her and said, "So, you and Kirsten…"

Andy had never told Seth about her personal life, having met with enough homophobia in the department and in the academy, so she was incredibly nervous when he said her girlfriend's name.

"What about me and Kirsten?" she said defensively.

"You're an item, right?"

Andy didn't know what to say. Should she deny it? Should she act offended? She had never been one to hide, but the guys in the Manchester Police Department weren't too accepting when it came to stuff like that. Seth's slightly sunburned face, his freckles out in full force, made Andy think of the innocence of childhood. There was nothing in his expression but curiosity— no sign of judgment or hatred.

"Yeah, so?" she asked gruffly, silently praying that she had made the right decision.

There was a long pause and then Seth smiled. "She's pretty hot."

Andy laughed and shoved him with her shoulder.

The memory brought tears to her eyes, and she felt as though she couldn't breathe. She pulled at the collar of her shirt.

Her thoughts were disrupted by the assistant director's bellowing voice: "Are you even listening to me, Cole?"

"Yes, sir!" she answered, snapping to attention.

"Parker from OCPD is running lead on the IA investigation. He'll debrief you. Now get out of my sight!"

* * *

Lexy had somehow managed to fall asleep in the uncomfortable plastic waiting room chair in the police station. When she awoke to the sound of her cell phone ringing, it took her a moment to figure out where she was.

"Hello?"

"Lexy, you sound awful." The warmth in Anna's voice instantly comforted her.

"I've been waiting here for…" She looked at the time on her phone display. "Jeez, close to an hour!" Lexy could hear Cayden shouting in the background, "Let me! Let me!"

"Someone wants to say hi…Hang on…" There was a rustling while the phone was passed to Cayden. From a distance, she heard Anna say, "Wrong end, silly!"

A few seconds later, Cayden's voice, bubbly and high-strung, shouted, "Hi!"

"Hi, handsome! How was the movie?"

"Great!" he yelled at the top of his lungs, which made Lexy yank the phone away from her ear. "'Cept when Buzz lost an arm!"

"Oh my goodness!" she said. "But he was okay, right?"

"Yeah." Cayden sounded as though he was chewing something.

"Are you guys eating dinner?"

"Yup! Mommy made bisgetty!"

"Yum!" Lexy said.

"Are you comin' over?" he asked.

"I don't know, Sweet Pea. Does your mommy want me to come over?"

She could hear Cayden drop the phone. There was the sound of scrambling as someone tried to pick it up.

When a voice finally returned, it was Anna's. "Sorry about that," she said.

"No problem."

"So, are you coming over tonight?"

Lexy smiled. "Do you want me to?"

"Yes."

"Then I'll be over as soon as I can."

"How's Jennifer?"

"Nobody'll tell me a thing. I've been sitting in the waiting room the entire time. How are you two?"

"Well, I know he doesn't sound it, but Cayden's probably heading to bed very soon." Lexy could hear him protest in the background.

"Oh," she said, disappointed. "I was hoping to catch at least part of a movie with you guys."

"Another day...for the movie, I mean, not for you coming over. I may not be Buzz Lightyear, but I'm sure I can find a way to entertain you."

Lexy laughed. "'To infinity and beyond.'"

\* \* \*

Adalia Johnson didn't recognize any of the women in the photographs that Officer Christopher Mackie had spread out before her. Unlike Detective Bunson, Mackie was in the traditional blue police uniform, all neatly tucked and polished. Adalia studied his red hair.

"You should try a hot oil treatment."

"What?" Officer Mackie looked up at her, squinting his right eye and scrunching his nose. "The women in the photos, ma'am, do any look familiar?"

None of the women had the features she remembered, the sharp jawline, the dark brooding eyes. She shook her head.

"Are you sure?" he asked.

"None of these are her. So, can we wrap this up now?"

"There is one other option, Ms. Johnson." Officer Mackie gathered the photos into a pile. "We'd like you to come to the station tomorrow morning and work with a sketch artist to produce a rendering of the woman that you saw."

Adalia sighed. She eyed the pile of photographs again, wishing that the woman's picture was in the stack so that she didn't have to return to this place. Its smell reminded her of dirty gym socks, and the uniforms, everything tucked in tightly and all the buckles shining, made her think of the Hitler shows on the History Channel. "I don't remember her too well."

"Oh yeah?" he said, smirking. "Well, we might suffer some amnesia ourselves and forget the details of that deal, Adalia."

Adalia didn't like the way that he said her name, stretching out the second syllable.

"Fine!" she snapped, imagining throwing her soda at him. She pictured the can hitting him in the eye and him being shocked and falling backward off his seat. Or better yet, the can could hit him dead center in the forehead. Thud. She smiled at the thought.

* * *

Andy Cole knocked on the glass wall that separated Chase Parker's office from the officers' stations.

Parker waved her in.

"Close the door behind you, Agent Cole."

Andy took the empty seat facing Parker's desk. She liked Detective Parker. He was one of the by-the-book guys, and there were few of those left. He was also a father of two. Andy had seen him and his boys at the OCPD Commendation Awards Luncheon, where one of her former colleagues was being awarded the medal of valor. She could see the hero worship in their eyes, and she knew that Parker was a good dad.

Detective Parker folded his hands in front of him. Andy felt like she was in the school principal's office awaiting punishment. "We've got a problem, don't we?" He didn't wait for a response before continuing. "We've interviewed Gardiner and she claims that you and she were involved. Intimately involved." He raised his eyebrows. "Would you like to dispute that?"

"No," Andy said solemnly.

"How long has this been going on?"

Andy felt like a frog in a dissection pan; she imagined that Parker was studying her reaction, facial expression, eye movements, etc. Which is exactly what she would be doing if the situation were reversed. "We weren't...involved until just after Labor Day." She fidgeted uncomfortably under his scrutiny.

"You weren't together then when you visited Key West to interview," he glanced down at the papers in front of him, "the Jensen girl?"

"No, I mean...well, we flirted, I guess."

"She says you were having problems just before she left for Marathon. Is that accurate?"

"We...um..." Andy bit her lip. "I was a little short with her. I guess you could say it was a problem...of sorts."

"You understand that I'll be forwarding this interview to FBI Headquarters and there will be an IA investigation?" he asked as he flipped open a spiral notepad with blue-lined paper.

"Yes. I understand." Andy's eyes fell on a five-by-seven framed photograph of Parker, his wife and their two sons. "You have a nice-looking family, Detective Parker."

"Thanks," he said and smiled proudly as his eyes fell on the photo. "Do you have a family, Cole?"

"No, I live alone." Andy hadn't seen her father since Seth's funeral. She would have been touched by the gesture, viewed it as empathy for her, had he not shown up drunk, stumbling and talking too loudly for the venue. Any love for her that might have motivated the trip was overshadowed by his blatant disregard for the solemnity of the occasion. He'd lost a partner early in his career as a beat cop in Charleston, and his trip was probably more about his pain than hers. It wasn't a surprise that he was drunk. He had been drunk practically every day since her mother had left them. A six-year-old Andy had watched through the banister as she walked out of their lives forever. Even now, the memory of the door slamming behind her mother made Andy flinch and her heart ache.

"I see," Parker said. Andy wasn't sure but she thought that she saw a quick glimmer of sympathy in his eyes. "So, why don't you explain from the beginning how you ended up in a relationship with this Jennifer Gardiner."

Andy talked and Parker took notes in his spiral notebook. Periodically during their discussion, Parker straightened his already straight tie; she'd seen some of her colleagues do this in the investigation room to send a signal to whoever was observing them through the double-sided mirror. But there was no mirror here. Andy turned to see if anyone was watching them, but there was no one there.

Parker would later transcribe the notes into an official report, which would then be sent to FBI Headquarters and Internal Affairs. Andy knew that she'd likely lose her job over this or at the very least be demoted. The IA investigation would probably drag on for weeks. She'd still collect paychecks, although she'd be chained to a desk for the entire time, processing paperwork and filling out reports. She couldn't bear to think of it. She loved being an FBI agent; in fact, it was the only thing about her life—aside from Jennifer—that made her happy.

# CHAPTER SIXTEEN

Lexy knocked lightly on Anna's door, not wanting to wake Cayden. The door opened to Anna wearing a satin nightgown and matching slippers. Her hair was loose and her face looked fresh as, though she had just washed it.

"I'm glad you came," she said.

Lexy liked the way the fabric of Anna's nightgown clung to her body when she moved, showing off her sexy curves.

"Cayden fell asleep as soon as his head hit the pillow. Tired out from intergalactic emergencies, I think."

Lexy let her body sink into the sofa cushions, massaging her neck with her fingers. "I can't believe I slept in that uncomfortable chair."

"Let me help." Anna began massaging the tight muscles of her shoulders.

"Mmmm. That feels good." Lexy relaxed into the feeling and closed her eyes.

"So still no news on Jennifer?"

"I left before she got out." Lexy didn't want to think about Jennifer right now; enjoying the feel of Anna's hands, which had moved to her neck. "I could get used to this," she said.

Lexy felt Anna's right hand shift some of Lexy's hair behind her ear. Then, her lips were on her neck.

A moan escaped Lexy's slightly parted lips.

Anna's mouth traveled up the side of Lexy's neck to her ear.

"I want you," Anna whispered. "I wish we could…My body doesn't seem to understand reason."

Lexy groaned in response. "I want you too," she breathed. "*So* much."

Anna's lips captured her mouth then, and her tongue seemed to Lexy to offer promises of amazing things to come.

They held each other for some time, Lexy's body desperately wanting and needing more.

"I guess it's time for me to go," Lexy finally said. Even if they couldn't be together intimately, she still didn't want to release her hold on the younger woman. She liked the way that Anna curled into her arms, her body melding into Lexy's. "I don't want to let go, Anna."

"I don't want you to." Anna pulled her tighter.

God, she loved this woman, Lexy thought. She loved the way that she felt in her arms. She loved the faint scent of vanilla in her hair, probably the fragrance of her shampoo. She loved the feel of her skin, warm, soft and inviting. She loved the way that she chewed on her pen caps in class. She even loved the way that her nose crinkled before she sneezed. She loved the warmth and heartfelt devotion in her eyes when she looked at her son. She loved the tiny gold flecks in her green irises. She *loved* this woman. She was *in love* with this woman.

What if Anna didn't feel the same? What if Lexy had been nothing more than a conquest to her? Eight years her senior and in a position of authority, Lexy might be a crush, a case of hero worship and nothing more. Surely Anna would want someone closer to her own age—someone young and vibrant. And Lexy knew full well that Anna could have women like that.

"Time for bed," she said, releasing her hold on Anna and pushing herself up off the couch.

Anna kissed her again at the door. "Sweet dreams, love," she said.

The word *love* and images of Anna lingered in Lexy's mind while she drifted off to sleep alone in her own bed.

# CHAPTER SEVENTEEN

By Wednesday afternoon, Cheryl Timber, a sketch artist at the Key West Police Department, had completed a composite of the mysterious woman to whom Adalia Johnson had given John Creighton's apartment number. Cheryl found Adalia difficult to work with—she had to be prodded for details and changed her mind repeatedly. She asked one last time if there was anything else that Adalia would change about the image to make it more accurate.

"No, that's her," she said. "That's definitely her!"

Cheryl always felt exceedingly satisfied when she heard similar phrases at the end of a long session with a difficult client. She unclipped the drawing Bristol paper from the Masonite board, collected her art gum eraser and graphite pencils and went in search of Detective Bunson. She disliked working with Bunson since he never failed to do something incredibly inappropriate, like patting her ass or talking to her breasts. She was relieved to find that he was in a meeting with the chief. Cheryl left the drawing on his desk and left the station in search of lunch.

* * *

Andy Cole shook hands with the FBI Internal Affairs investigator, a pretty brunette with a nice figure who introduced herself as Rebecca Sheffield.

"Can I call you Andrea?" she asked.

"I prefer Andy."

"Andy then." Rebecca smiled. "So, let's have a seat." Andy sat, as directed, in the only other chair in the room. "As I'm sure you're aware, this conversation will be videotaped for your protection." The video camera sat atop a tripod in the corner of the room, its lens focused on Andy.

Andy had thought that the investigator's questions would pertain to her relationship with Jennifer, and some did, but she was also asked to recount the day that she visited the Blue Parrot Apartment Complex.

"Did you drive or fly to Key West?"

"I drove my Jeep."

"And at what time did you leave?"

Andy thought back to that Saturday morning. She remembered that she had gotten up early for her run. She'd packed a duffel bag with a change of clothes and assorted toiletries. She didn't bother with breakfast since she had decided to stop at a convenience store on the way and pick up a protein bar or something. "I was on the road by seven."

"And you arrived at...?"

The trip from Orlando to Key West normally took seven hours. Although Andy knew she'd need to stop for gas and something to eat along the way, she had expected to be there by two o'clock. But then there was construction and traffic. "A quarter to three."

"And then?"

"I stopped for a bite at a place called Pete's Patio Bar and Grill." She remembered the umbrellaed tables out front. "I grabbed a twenty and left my wallet in the glove box. I was just going to order a sandwich to go."

The inside of the restaurant had reminded Andy of the old-time piano bars and lounges, with its wraparound leather couches and deep red tablecloths and carpet. The bar was U-shaped and the stools were filled with patrons. She spotted a stack of paper menus at the bar register and immediately headed in its direction. Under the bar's clear-coat countertop were photographs of various people having fun drinking, some dressed in funny costumes at some sort of event. She was looking at a photo of a man in a gorilla suit when the woman behind the counter asked her a question.

"You want a drink, hon?" she asked, wiping down the bar with a wet rag.

"No, I was hoping to order a sandwich to go."

"Well, we've got plenty of those. I like the Big Bird, myself." She passed Andy one of the paper menus.

"So I was standing there looking over the menu," Andy explained, "when the TV in the corner of the bar grabs my attention—some news broadcast, MSNBC maybe. It was something about a cop breaking up a fight between a couple teenagers. But it was hard to hear on account of the guy on the stool next to me pounding on a ketchup bottle and cursing under his breath. I saw the reporter on the television point down an alley and say something like, 'Here's where the shooting took place.'" Andy shivered. "And that's when I felt it—something hit the side of my face. And when I reached up to wipe it off, my fingers came away red. The next thing I know," Andy shook her head, "I'm waking up on some beach and it's going on four."

"What did you do then?" the investigator asked.

"When I couldn't find my car, I flagged down a taxi and had the guy take me back to Pete's. My Jeep was right where I remembered leaving it in the parking lot. And that's when I drove to the Blue Parrot."

"And what time did you arrive there?"

"Four thirty."

"So you have no recollection of your whereabouts between two forty-five and four?"

"No, I honestly don't." Andy realized that this sounded bad; in fact, if she were Rebecca Sheffield, she wouldn't believe her story. "My partner died in a similar shooting, and I've been seeing a therapist ever since. Although they aren't common, I've had blackouts before."

\* \* \*

On Wednesday, Jennifer and Lexy met for lunch off campus at a little diner they frequented.

"So?" Lexy said, peeling the wrapper from her straw. "What happened?"

"They found a Key West receipt, but it wasn't mine." Jennifer took a bite of her burger and wiped the leftover barbecue sauce from her lip with her napkin.

Lexy sprinkled salt on her fries. She knew she shouldn't be eating them, but when Jennifer ordered her cheeseburger with bacon and a side of fried onions, Lexy's mouth had watered, refusing to be satisfied unless it got something fried or fattening. "So you're not an actual suspect, right?"

"Well, not anymore," Jennifer said after swallowing. She took a sip of her soda. "But Andy's being questioned now."

"*Andy*? What the hell does she have to do with anything?"

"Well, it turns out that she's not a professor at all. She's an undercover FBI agent." Jennifer said this so nonchalantly that Lexy wasn't sure if she had heard her correctly.

"She's a *what*?"

Jennifer wiped her mouth with her paper napkin. "The detective told me that she was planted at the college as part of some task force investigating the murders...*and me*."

"You have *got* to be kidding!" This sounded to Lexy like the plot of one of Jennifer's pulpy mystery thrillers.

"'Fraid not. I guess they've got some kind of investigation now into her involvement with me."

"What involvement?"

"We've been sleeping together."

"*Oh my god!*" Lexy was beside herself with shock.

"And, man, is she hot in bed!" Jennifer smiled in such a way that Lexy was sure she was reviewing the "hot" details in her head.

"So you were being investigated for the murders and you slept with the agent investigating you?"

"Looks like it."

Lexy's head was starting to hurt.

"So, what's new with you?" Jennifer laughed, taking a bite out of an onion ring.

\* \* \*

At the Tampa field office, Patrick Reilly was writing up a report on an online predator who had been booked that afternoon, when his admin dropped the fax on his desk.

"A suspect in the Jensen murder," she said and trotted off.

Reilly read the cover page, which had been prepared by a Detective Bunson of the Key West Police Department. Included was a short description of the Adalia Johnson interview. Reilly flipped the page to the sketch.

It took only a second for the dark eyes, the jet-black hair, the strong features to register. It was definitely Andy Cole.

# CHAPTER EIGHTEEN

When she'd heard the knock on her apartment door, Andy had just begun stretching after her run.

"Andy Cole, you are under arrest for the murder of Samantha Jensen." Detective Parker secured the handcuffs.

She couldn't believe this was happening. When Parker had asked her to submit to a DNA swab, she'd agreed without hesitation, thinking that it could do nothing but clear her. But it obviously hadn't. *Why hadn't it?*

Even though she had blacked out, she knew she couldn't possibly have been involved. She wasn't capable of mutilating a woman or of killing a person in anything but self-defense. And she wasn't even sure if she could kill in self-defense since, thank god, she'd never had to fire her weapon in the line of duty. She had drawn her weapon twice, once when she was confronted with a drunk and disorderly flailing a carving knife about and once when Seth was shot. Well, she assumed that she pulled her weapon; she had practically no memory of the actual shooting.

The kid must have disarmed her in some sort of a struggle, though, since it was her gun that he had used to shoot Seth.

No, she certainly couldn't do what they were accusing her of. And where the *hell* was Jennifer? She hadn't seen her since they'd taken her in for questioning the previous week, even though she'd left multiple messages on her voice mail. She had wanted to explain since she knew that Jennifer would be told that she was working undercover. "Look, somebody's messed up here! It's not me. For Christ's sake! Parker! You know me!"

"You have the right to remain silent. Anything you say…" Detective Parker led her to the police cruiser idling just outside her apartment.

* * *

When Anna returned to Lexy's Beetle from dropping Cayden off at First Steps Preschool, she had tears in her eyes. She said nothing while she took her seat and adjusted the shoulder strap of her seat belt.

Cayden, whom she had signed up for morning sessions five days a week, nine to one, hadn't experienced as difficult a transition as she had. For the first two sessions, Anna refused to leave and watched Cayden the entire time. She had only agreed to go home on the third day at the urging of Dr. Breck, the psychologist she'd consulted at the Family Center, and the teachers' agreement to send regular text message updates to her phone.

She was pleasantly surprised to see how easily Cayden made friends. She watched him offer the blond boy next to him his crayons, and she was proud to see how willing he was to share. He also seemed to have no trouble falling into the daily schedule of lessons, arts and crafts and naps, and he was very polite with the teachers, always saying "thank you" and "please." She suspected that Ian was responsible for his good manners.

"It's okay," Lexy said, giving Anna's thigh a squeeze.

"They were singing the teapot song when I left," Anna said solemnly, punching the preset radio station buttons on the dash.

* * *

"How about I make you breakfast?"

"Okay." Anna wiped at her eyes with the back of her hand.

Anna watched as Lexy added some chopped Vidalia onion, yellow pepper and plum tomatoes to a heated pan. She then turned her attention to the eggs.

The heavenly aroma that filled the kitchen while Lexy worked over the stovetop made Anna's stomach growl. She busied herself with the task of trying to figure out how to work the French press that Lexy had pushed in her direction when she asked where the coffeemaker was. "Maybe I'll make tea—something less complicated," she said, turning the French press over in her hand and inspecting it as though it were some alien contraption.

"I'll do it, sweetie. You stir my concoction."

Anna liked being called "sweetie." It made her feel like they were together. A couple. She stirred the delicious-looking breakfast with the wooden spoon she found resting on the granite countertop next to the pan. "I like that."

Lexy poured the water into the press. "What?"

"That you called me sweetie."

She pushed in the plunger and smiled.

"The past couple weeks, Lexy, you've been so great with Cayden. He just adores you!"

Lexy came behind Anna and kissed her neck. "How about his mother?" she asked.

"She adores you too." Anna leaned her head back on Lexy's chest and felt the woman's fingers comb through her hair.

After breakfast, the two women went out on the back patio to finish their coffee.

"Do you have to go into work today? I'd love it if you'd spend the day with us."

"Well, it's a faculty workday, but nobody really keeps tabs on who's there." Lexy set her coffee on the bistro table and sat in one of the Adirondack chairs. Anna positioned herself between Lexy's legs and leaned her head back on her shoulder.

"Anna?"

"Yeah?" Anna, feeling incredibly content in Lexy's arms, allowed her eyes to close.

"I'm not just a conquest, am I?"

"A *conquest*?" she asked, opening her eyes.

"You know—a crush or something. It's pretty common, developing a crush on a teacher or authority figure…"

Anna turned around to face her, her legs straddling the chair. "You think I have a schoolgirl crush?"

Lexy shrugged her shoulders in response.

"This isn't a crush or a conquest. I want to be with you for more than just a passionate night. I want to be *with* you." She couldn't tell from Lexy's expression if she believed her. "God, Lex, I want a relationship with you—not just sex!"

Lexy smiled. "So you don't find me attractive then?" she asked coyly.

Anna slid closer. She pressed her lips to Lexy's neck. "I've never been more attracted to any woman than you," she whispered. Lexy shivered in response.

Anna kissed her lips then, deeply and passionately. She could feel Lexy's hips begin to move in slow circles. "Where's your bedroom?" she asked.

In the bedroom, Anna lifted her shirt over her head, revealing the print push-up bra she'd chosen because of the way it accentuated her cleavage. The hungry expression in Lexy's eyes emboldened her to make a show of unbuttoning the button fly of her jeans.

Lexy, watching intently, followed suit and unbuttoned her own blouse. She let the fabric fall from her shoulders.

Anna couldn't bear to not touch her. Leaving her jeans on but unfastened, she approached Lexy and kissed from her neck to her collarbone. She could see Lexy's pulse quicken in the side of her neck and she could feel her body respond to the touch of her lips. She let her hand roam lightly over Lexy's stomach and settle on her breasts, her nipples hardening to the touch. Anna unclasped Lexy's bra with her other hand and let it drop to the floor, revealing deep-pink erect nipples and firm breasts. "So beautiful," she said, taking in her body.

"Please, I want to feel you," Lexy begged.

"Undress me then."

Lexy undid the front clasp of Anna's bra and slid the straps off her shoulders. She pulled Anna to her and kissed her greedily then, sucking her bottom lip into her mouth. Anna felt Lexy's hands slide between them, touching her breasts, squeezing her nipples lightly at first and then more firmly. Anna's body responded immediately, and the feeling that began in her breasts coursed through her and settled between her legs. "God," she breathed into Lexy's mouth. "So good," Anna managed. She could barely find the words, her mind completely consumed by the jolts of arousal that Lexy milked from her with her experienced fingers.

Anna arched her back in invitation, and Lexy took a nipple in her mouth, sucking lightly, raking her teeth over its surface.

Anna frantically grabbed at Lexy's shorts, yanking at the button and zipper. She knew it was fast. She knew she should take her time, but she couldn't stop herself. She needed to feel her. She needed to be inside her. She pushed the silky panties aside and slipped a finger through her folds—over her swollen clit. Lexy gasped.

Anna could feel Lexy's fingers slip underneath the waistband of her jeans. She moaned into Lexy's neck as she felt those fingers caress her. "You're so wet," Lexy said as she entered her.

Anna was already climbing toward orgasm herself and suddenly feared that she would climax too soon. She stopped Lexy's hand by closing her fingers around her wrist.

"I want to taste you," Anna said as she stripped Lexy of her shorts and panties and replaced her hand with her mouth. She slid her tongue through her folds, elated by the wetness that greeted her.

"Oh god," Lexy breathed. Anna continued to kiss and suck her clit as she plunged her fingers inside her. "Yes," Lexy said. "Anna! Yes!" Her voice was louder now. Anna could feel the muscles contract around her fingers. "YES!" Lexy's voice was a shout now as her body bucked against Anna's hand.

Anna waited for Lexy's body to still, for the last tremors to pass, before climbing up to face her. "God, you're beautiful," she said and kissed her softly on the lips. Lexy deepened the kiss, her tongue sliding into Anna's mouth, while her hands worked to rid her of what clothing she still had on.

Lexy lifted Anna's knee over her shoulder, leaving Anna feeling exposed—thrillingly exposed—to the cool, air-conditioned air.

Anna's eyes slammed shut when she felt a finger push inside her and then another—filling her, taking her. And when they disappeared, she whimpered at their absence. "Please?" she heard herself beg. Lexy lifted her other leg over her shoulder and cupped her ass in her hands. *My god*, Anna thought, as she felt the heat of Lexy's breath on her sex. She spiraled toward orgasm as Lexy made love to her with her tongue, with her lips, plunging in and out of her and then stopping to slide over her clit, to suck her clit into her mouth. Anna lost all sense of what was happening, what Lexy was doing to her, and just surrendered to the feeling. The mounting pressure inside her was almost too much to bear. She could feel a wrenching scream rising to the surface and she buried her face in the pillow.

She shook, her whole body shook, racked with pleasure, as the scream escaped her. It sounded foreign to her ears as if it came from some wild animal instead of from a woman, from her.

Anna's eyes opened to find Lexy watching her, her lashes wet with tears.

"I love you," Lexy said and then immediately turned away. "God, I'm sorry, that was way too fast." Lexy shook her head, her eyes fixed on the wall. "I'm a bad joke—the U-Haul lesbian." She laughed a self-deprecating laugh that twisted Anna's stomach in knots.

"Lexy?" Anna waited for the woman to turn her face to her before she said it. "I love you too."

* * *

Andy learned during the first round of questions in the investigation room that the clerk at the Blue Parrot placed her at the scene during her blackout—a little after three, with the time of death marked as three thirty. She also learned that DNA evidence proved that the earring was hers, with 99.93 percent accuracy. This was perhaps the most damning piece of evidence. Andy knew that there had to be a logical explanation. She just didn't know what it was.

She thought of Jennifer as her eyes fell on the blue sky through the bars in the cell window. By now, she had probably been told who Andy was and why she was there at the college. If so, she'd be furious with her. And what if they'd told her about the earring at the crime scene and the clerk's testimony? Andy shivered at the thought. All that didn't keep her stubborn brain from thinking it might be Jennifer when she'd been told that she had a visitor. It wasn't. It was Patrick Reilly.

Reilly had visited Pete's Patio Bar and Grill and had taken pictures of the parking lot, the inside bar and the tables and booths, hoping to jog Andy's memory. Looking over the photos on his iPad, Andy instantly recognized the place—the loungy feel of the booths and the heavily varnished bar with the photographs, the gorilla costume. She recalled stepping up to the register at the bar and looking over a take-out menu. The television, the report of a cop being shot, the balding guy trying to get ketchup out of the bottle. He must have sprayed her with it. She remembered feeling it on her face and seeing it on her hands.

"That accounts for the mysterious red stains that the clerk claims she saw on your shirt sleeve," Reilly said. "The blackout was probably triggered by seeing what your brain took in as blood on your hands—that, combined with the story of the cop being shot, could've brought back the trauma of Seth's shooting," he said.

"But where do we go from here?" she asked. "My wallet was in the Jeep when I got back to it, so I had nothing to remind me who I was, just a twenty and Samantha Jensen's name and the Blue Parrot address scrawled on a piece of scrap paper. You suppose I went to the apartment complex, thinking that's where I was staying?"

"You would have had to have taken a taxi. The Blue Parrot is at least a ten-minute drive from the restaurant, and your car was parked in the exact same spot you left it, right?"

"Maybe you should see if anyone at the taxi service remembers me?"

"Good idea, and I'll review Adalia Johnson and her cousin's testimony too. See if I can find anything."

"Thank you for believing in me, Patrick." Her eyes grew watery as she tried to hold back her tears.

"No problem, partner." He winked at her and smiled.

* * *

Cayden excitedly told Lexy about the paper airplanes that they made at preschool that day. He held one in his hand and flew it around Lexy's arm, making engine sounds as he did. Anna watched the two interact and imagined what it might be like if the three of them made a home together. Lexy picked Cayden up in the air and pretended to throw him, shouting, "One... Two...Three!" At the count of three, she whisked his body high into the air, never actually letting go, and then brought the giggling boy back down again onto the asphalt driveway.

"Let's watch *Monsters, Inc.*!" he shouted.

"We've seen that one five times." Anna poked her nose into his.

"I would love to see that again! Am I invited?" Lexy wrapped an arm around Anna and almost kissed her cheek. Anna had made it clear that she didn't want them to show affection around Cayden until they were more certain of their relationship. Lexy was having trouble keeping her hands to herself.

"We could have a slumber party!" Anna said, suddenly excited. "We could watch movies, eat popcorn and play a couple games of Candy Land!" She turned to Cayden. "What do you think, champ? Can Lexy stay over with us?"

Cayden leaped at Lexy, wrapping his arms around her waist and burying his face in her stomach. "Slumber party!" he shouted.

"I guess that's a yes." Anna smiled.

* * *

Jennifer sat down at her writing desk, opened her laptop and pressed the on button. She felt inspired and knew exactly where her new manuscript would be heading. The first thing she did was highlight the title and press delete, and the second was to change her main character's occupation from bartender to cop. "Why, Angie," she whispered, "you've been a very bad girl."

* * *

Anna and Lexy sat on opposite sides of Cayden on the small loveseat in Anna's living room. A big bowl of buttered popcorn rested in Anna's lap, and Lexy secretly liked having to reach over into the younger woman's lap to grab handfuls of the snack.

Cayden was singing along with the monsters on the screen. His eyelids were slightly droopy and he was no longer swinging his arms or clapping his hands. Lexy knew that meant that he'd be asleep in less than an hour.

Lexy stretched her arm along the back of the couch and rested her hand on Anna's shoulder.

"Mommy?" Cayden asked. "Do you have a boyfriend like Daddy?"

Anna reddened slightly. "No, honey."

"Are you gonna?" No longer interested in the monsters, Cayden turned his full attention to his mother.

"No, Cayden, I'm not."

"Why?"

"Because, honey, Mommy doesn't want a boyfriend." Anna roped her fingers through his.

"Do you kiss boys?" he asked.

"What's with all the questions, pumpkin?"

"Well, Daddy said that you're a Libyan."

"I'm from Libya?"

Lexy laughed. "I think he means lesbian."

"Yeah!" Cayden shouted.

"Oh, well, that's true. Mommy dates girls instead of boys."

"How come?" Ginger licked Cayden's bare foot, making him giggle.

"How 'bout we save that conversation for another day, huh, tiger?"

"Do you and Lexy like each other?" he asked.

Lexy and Anna exchanged surprised expressions. "Um. Yeah. Lexy and I like each other."

"Do you kiss each other like Daddy and Christian?"

"Yes, Cayden, we kiss each other."

He seemed to consider this for a moment and sat silently, playing with a string that hung from the hem of his shirt. "Do you love each other?"

Anna swallowed. "Yes, Cayden, we love each other."

"Then how come you don't live together?" he asked.

"Good question, Cayden." Lexy smiled at Anna. *Maybe we will someday soon.*

# CHAPTER NINETEEN

Reilly visited two cab companies, Yellow Cab and Red Top, before he finally tracked down a driver who recognized Andy's picture. The chain-smoking guy in the derby hat immediately knew who she was when his eyes fell on the black-and-white photograph of Cole. "I didn't know she was FBI," he said, blowing out two clouds of smoke through his nostrils. "She didn't seem like it." Reilly coughed, his throat and eyes irritated by the smoke.

"What can you tell me about her? How was she acting?"

"She seemed out of it—like weird. She asked me where she was and when I told her the street name, it was like it didn't register."

"Did she tell you where she wanted to go?"

"No, she just pushed a piece of paper at me and I took her to the address on it. It was the Blue Parrot in Key West. She stiffed me on the tip."

"But she paid you?"

"She gave me a twenty and took all the change."

"So you dropped her off at the Blue Parrot. What did she do then?"

"Well, I saw her just sort of look around, you know, like she didn't recognize the place. Then she made her way over to the main lobby. I don't know after that cuz I took off."

* * *

Dr. Lenar, Andy's psychiatrist, and her lawyer sat across from her at a table in the visiting room.

"I just want to find the lost time." Andy reached across the table and grasped Dr. Lenar's hand as if trying to keep the woman from leaving despite the fact that she had only just arrived.

"No touching," the uniformed guard said curtly.

Releasing her grasp, Andy pleaded, "I could know something that could help the case, something that could help them find the real killer."

"Well, hypnosis has been used as a retrieval method." She studied Andy's expression, and after a beat, added, "With mixed results. Don't misunderstand. Hypnosis doesn't stand up in court, but it might help you recover some of the repressed memories. I have a colleague who specializes in hypnotherapy. I could ask him to—"

"Yes!" Andy exclaimed, eyes wide and head nodding excitedly. "Please, ask him."

* * *

Lexy and Rand sat at the bistro table in Lexy's backyard sharing a bottle of cabernet. She was on her second glass, so she felt calm and slightly warm inside.

"So, how did Ari make it up to you?"

Rand sipped his wine, his pinky extended as he gripped the stem between his thumb and index finger. "The usual— jewelry." He showed off a new broad-band titanium ring with a dark gemstone in the center. "Followed by plenty of groveling, expensive flowers and good sex, of course."

"You're not mad anymore?" Lexy searched the stars for Anna's Andromeda.

"No. I love him. And I know he loves me. Even if he is *stupid* sometimes."

Having found the constellation, she traced the stick-figure warrior with her finger. "I'm thinking about asking Anna to move in."

"Wow!" Rand's eyelids shot open in surprise. "That's pretty serious. How long before you and Jules got a place together?"

Her mind conjured the memory of Jules filling the bookshelves of that little upstairs apartment they'd rented in Portland, Maine. Rather than organize them alphabetically or by genre, Jules had arranged the books by height, with the taller ones on the left and the shorter on the right. Anytime Lexy would search for a book, she would, following the height of the spines, subconsciously tilt her head to the right. She smiled at the memory. "We dated for close to a year before moving in together," she said. "Do you think it's too fast—for Anna and me?"

"Well, you have to be sure. Children get attached."

"I know. But I love Cayden," she said matter-of-factly. "And the second bedroom is the perfect size for him." She hugged her knees to her chest, feeling a slight chill from the wind. "How should I ask her?"

"You could send her a singing telegram." He laughed. "Or a singing drag queen."

"I was thinking a little less...dramatic."

"I don't know, Hon, but you'll know when the moment's right."

* * *

Lexy invited Anna and Cayden over to the condo the following evening for dinner. She made Cayden's favorite, meat loaf and mashed potatoes, and some steamed broccoli for his mother.

"This looks so good!" Anna said, smiling at her full plate.

Cayden stuck his finger in his pile of mashed potatoes. Anna sighed. "Sweetie, please use the spoon." She cleaned off his finger with her napkin.

"How was school today?" Lexy asked.

Cayden, who had already shoveled a rather large spoonful of potatoes into his mouth, tried to answer, but his words came out muffled and incoherent. A small flurry of white flecks of potato flew from his mouth like tiny snowballs.

"Honey, chew first and then answer," Anna said.

He chewed for what seemed like an impossibly long time, swallowed and then said, "I know the alphabet song!"

"You do?"

"A, b, c, d, e, f, g…" he sang.

"You should start saving for Harvard." Lexy winked at Anna, who smiled proudly.

After dinner, Lexy offered to give the two a tour of the condo. Anna had already seen almost everything, preferring to spend her time in the master bedroom than any other room in the house, of course, but Lexy had ulterior motives for the tour. She wanted to show Anna the size of the guest bedroom in the hopes that she might be able to convince her that it would be perfect for Cayden.

"What's that room?" Anna asked, noticing that Lexy didn't identify one of the closed doors as they walked through the hallway.

"That's storage. I keep my sculptures in there."

"Can we see?" she asked.

Lexy was nervous about the prospect of Anna recognizing herself in her most recent work. Would she think that she was some desperate woman—that she was obsessive? A stalker? "Um…I…I'm not sure if you should."

"Don't be embarrassed, Lex, I'm sure we'll love your sculptures. Won't we, handsome?"

Cayden was disinterested in the room and in his mother at the moment. He was playing with a Matchbox car, driving it along the wall.

Lexy took a deep breath and turned the doorknob.

She watched Anna walk toward the metal shelves that lined the far wall. Each was filled with pottery, mostly bowls of different sizes with intricate leaf or tribal designs. Anna picked up one of the glazed pieces, a pitcher, and turned it around in her fingers. Lexy watched as she ran her index finger along the ribbed surface and over the grooves where the glaze had gathered. "How pretty!" she said. "You should use these."

"They're Jules's. I'm not very good at the wheel."

"Oh." Anna carefully placed the pitcher back in its spot and then put her hands in her pockets, as if she were afraid to handle them.

"I don't know why I keep them hidden in here," Lexy said. "I really should put them out where people can appreciate them."

"Which ones are yours?"

Lexy pointed to the pieces on the adjacent wall and watched Anna's eyes, following the gesture, take in the female figures on the bottom shelf. Anna walked closer and crouched down. The nudes ranged in size from half a foot in height to two feet tall. Anna reached out to touch one—a sculpture of a pregnant woman with long hair that stretched to her waist.

Lexy nervously bit at her nail as Anna approached the table under the far window where she housed her most recent pieces. They were all of Anna in different positions—some made out of red clay and some of white. As Lexy watched Anna study the figures, her heart raced. Anna turned to face her then, her eyes brimming with tears. "They're me?" she asked.

Unable to speak, Lexy nodded.

"But how did you know what my body looked like?"

"I didn't." She shrugged. "I guess I just imagined." She swallowed hard and felt nervousness flare in her stomach.

Anna turned back to the figures. "They're beautiful," she said, her fingers closing around one of the figure's hips.

"Do you think they lack substance?"

"What?"

"Someone told me once that my art lacked emotion."

"God no! They're full of emotion," Anna said. "I love them. *Really*." She smiled. "Can I have one for my apartment?"

"Actually, that's something I wanted to talk to you about." Lexy took her hand and led her to the next room. Opening wide the door to the guest room, Lexy said, "This could be a good kid's room, don't you think?"

Anna turned questioning eyes on Lexy.

"I know it's fast, Anna, but I also know that I love you and I love Cayden. I want to come home to you in the evenings. I want to curl up with you at night in our bed. I want to grow old with you. And I want to see Cayden grow up...here, with you and me." The words fell out of her in a jumbled mess, not at all how she'd imagined.

Anna wrapped her arms around Lexy's neck and kissed her. "I love you, Lexy Strayer, and I think this would be a perfect room for Cayden!" she said.

Lexy couldn't remember a time that she felt so happy, so complete and so wonderfully fulfilled.

# CHAPTER TWENTY

Moving day was a busy one. Anna was surprised that she was able to fill the van with the things she'd collected over the years. The van was probably only slightly smaller than her entire apartment.

Anna was incredibly happy to be moving in with Lexy, and although she was a little worried about uprooting Cayden so soon after he'd arrived, he seemed perfectly content. In fact, at the moment, he was having fun directing Lexy on which boxes to take in first. She was surprised by the patience the woman showed while following her son's absurd rules. In order to play this game, and Anna could see that it was, in fact, a game, Lexy had to point to a box and wait for Cayden to shake his head yes or no. And if he shook no, she would have to move on to another box. Seeing that this game could possibly go on forever and knowing that they only had the van rental until noon the following day, Anna picked up her son and placed him on her shoulders. "I need your help, little man," she said as she deposited him in the back of the van and climbed in after him. "I need your strength. Do you think you can help Mommy?"

* * *

As Lexy unloaded the boxes from the van, she remembered when she had driven Jules and all of their furniture in the rented Budget truck all the way from Portland, Maine, to Orlando, Florida. Lexy hadn't ever driven a truck before and she had not been successful in identifying the switch to turn on the headlights. Since it was approaching sundown, both she and Jules stared cockeyed and upside down at the many diagrams in the truck manual. It was Jules who finally found the headlight switch. Lexy thought to herself now that it was Jules who usually solved their problems. In the process of finding the information about the switch, she had read something about pressing a "toggle." Neither Lexy nor Jules had the foggiest idea of what a toggle was, but the notice in the manual pertaining to it sounded important enough for them to find it.

Jules decided that the small metal button next to the clutch was the mysterious toggle, and, as the manual suggested, she directed Lexy to press it any time she was traveling uphill. About fifty miles into the trip, they would come to realize that the metal button was not in fact the toggle; but was the switch to turn the high beam lights on. They had been flashing drivers for almost an hour, which would explain the random honking and lewd gestures that they received along the way.

It seemed that they were destined for trouble on that trip. A shortcut led them to a bridge that had a weight limit written in kilograms. Lexy pulled off to the side as they contemplated the conversion from kilograms to pounds. The map revealed no alternative route. They had already come some twenty-five miles on the shortcut, and there was no way she was willing to backtrack and add time to the trip.

"Well, what do you think?" Lexy's eyes fell on her partner, who unfortunately looked just as confused as she was. The stick of a Tootsie Pop she had purchased on their last stop was poking out of her mouth, and Lexy thought she looked adorable.

"How should I know?" she asked, shrugging her shoulders.

"You're the one who got a seven hundred on your math SAT, right? I'm an English teacher, so I'm excused."

"Lexy, that was over ten years ago!"

They both looked at each other, looked in the rearview mirror to see how far they'd come, looked at the water down below, and finally looked back at the sign. Jules crossed her fingers, and Lexy stepped on the gas, being sure to press the metal button in the floorboard as they were about to travel uphill. "A toggle for good luck," she said, smiling at Jules.

Lexy, who was currently struggling under the weight of a large box marked "Kitchen," turned to Anna now and asked, "Do you know what a toggle is?"

"No clue." Anna was passing Cayden a tennis racket from the van so that he could feel as though he was helping. "Should I?"

Cayden must have liked the sound of the word *toggle* because he started repeating it like a mantra until the words melted together into some sort of Gregorian chant sounding song: "Toggletoggletoggletoggle!"

"How about kilograms and pounds?"

Anna jumped down out of the back of the van. "I know they exist. What about them?"

"Do you know how to convert from one to the other?"

Anna smiled. "I know a tablespoon is three teaspoons. Does that help?"

"Come here." She pulled Anna to her in a warm hug. "It's perfect." Lexy couldn't help but think that Jules would approve of the leap of faith that she had taken in asking Anna and Cayden to move in with her. She felt like she was pressing the gas pedal now and gunning the truck over that bridge. She was directing her life, just like Jules had instructed her to do.

* * *

It was evening and sheets of rain were batting against the windows. Lightning lit up the sky in violent flashes. The storm had come on suddenly, which is common in Florida. Cayden grew almost as frightened as Ginger, who had buried herself in Lexy's laundry basket. Only her shaking tail was visible. Cayden had begun to cry after the first crack of thunder, which was so loud that Anna herself had jumped. Lexy pulled Cayden into her lap on the couch. When the lights and the television went out, Cayden burrowed into Lexy's chest, his crying so violent that she felt her shirt grow wet with his tears.

"It's just the angels," Lexy said, smoothing his hair, which was sticking to his forehead with perspiration. "They're playing telephone and they have to shout really loudly."

At first she didn't think he'd heard, but then his face lifted so that she could see his green eyes and wet lashes. "Have you ever played telephone?"

He shook his head.

"Well, that's what we should do, build ourselves a telephone like the angels!"

Cayden looked at his mother then, and she smiled reassuringly, as if to say she completely agreed.

Lexy stood, holding Cayden to her chest, and carried him to the kitchen. She grabbed a bag of paper cups from the cupboard and some string and tape from the junk drawer.

By the time Lexy had rigged two cups to the ends of a four-foot length of string, Cayden seemed to have completely forgotten about the storm raging outside. Lexy took one of the cups and put it up to her ear. "Well, let's try it out. Say something in your end."

He picked up the cup attached to the other end, and although he was still sitting in Lexy's lap, he yelled, "Hello!" into its center.

"Are you trying to blow my eardrum out?" she asked, which caused him to giggle. "Now, you go over there," she pointed to the cupboard, "and say something into your phone."

Cayden leaped off her lap and ran for the cupboard. He hid himself behind the cupboard door. "Don't look!" he shouted at her. "Hi, Lexy!" he said into the cup.

"Hi, Cayden!" she said back.

He was laughing now. "I want to make one!" he said, returning to the table.

Lexy showed a very happy Cayden how to attach the string to the cup with some tape. Not that either of them would have noticed, being so busy enjoying each other's company, but the storm had since cleared and the electricity had been restored.

# CHAPTER TWENTY-ONE

Andy's eyes rolled beneath her lids as if she were in a deep sleep.

"Andy, can you still hear me?" Dr. Mohanti asked in the same soothing voice he had used for the guided relaxation exercises.

"Yes," Andy mumbled.

"Good. So let's continue. You are standing at the counter of Pete's Patio Bar and Grill and are looking over the menu when you hear a news report on television. What is the newscaster saying?"

"A shooting…'officer down.'" Andy's words were uttered so softly that both Dr. Mohanti and Dr. Lenar had to lean in to hear her.

"Only a couple drinks…I'm *fine*."

Dr. Mohanti turned searching eyes on his colleague. She raised her eyebrows and shrugged her shoulder in response. "Andy, who are you talking to? The waitress?"

"I'll cover the back," she said, ignoring his question. The rhythm of the agent's heartbeat in her neck noticeably quickened.

Dr. Lenar, realizing that Andy was reliving a different moment but thinking that this was the perfect opportunity to help the woman work through the issues at the root of her troubles, made a rolling motion with her finger to prompt her colleague to continue. He nodded.

"Andy, you're safe and nothing can hurt you. Do you understand?"

"Yes."

"Can you describe what you see?"

\* \* \*

Andy lost sight of her partner as he rounded the side of the house. The reach of the streetlights stopped at the sidewalk, so she pulled the long metal flashlight from its holster as she walked along the perimeter in the opposite direction. She flicked the switch on the flashlight. Nothing. She shook it and tried again. Still nothing. *Damn it.* She peered through a window but it was too dark to see. Remembering her training, she mentally catalogued the doors, windows and exit routes.

Her heart leapt at the sound of glass shattering. There was a commotion inside the house. Someone was yelling. *Was that Seth's voice?* She ran to the nearest door but found it locked. She smashed the door handle with her flashlight several times before the screws came loose and the handle fell to the floor. Putting all of her body weight into it, she slammed her shoulder into the door, splintering the wood. She was through.

With her heart pounding and her gun drawn, she ran toward where she thought the sound had originated.

There was a blur of movement up ahead, but she couldn't make out any distinctive shapes. And suddenly there was a tall dark figure running straight for her. With shaky hands, she raised her weapon. It was coming too fast. There was no time.

It would be upon her in a second. She opened her mouth to say something, but the words didn't come. She fired. Something warm hit the exposed skin of her face and neck. The figure fell heavily to the floor.

A sound of something moving behind her pulled her attention away from the figure on the floor. She reacted quickly, managing to grab hold of the young man's jacket and wrestle him to the ground.

The kid showed little resistance as she closed the plastic restraints around his wrists. In fact, he looked scared.

After she was sure that she had him subdued, she cautiously approached the other figure. It wasn't moving.

\* \* \*

"Oh my god!" Andy cried out in a strangled voice. Her voice was so jarring that Rosemary Lenar actually jumped in her seat. The officers on guard responded by reaching for their batons.

"You're safe, Andy. Remember, you're safe. Nothing can hurt you," Dr. Mohanti repeated.

Tears streamed down the woman's cheeks. "I didn't mean to do it!" she shrieked. "It was a mistake!"

\* \* \*

It was the morning of Andy's arraignment. Reilly had been unable to trace her trail past the front door of Apartment 12A. She'd been seen knocking on the door at approximately 3:20 p.m. on September 5 by a member of the custodial staff at the Blue Parrot. The time fit with the information presented in Adalia Johnson's interview. But then the trail went cold until she reappeared to find the body. There was nothing more.

The earring, as well as eyewitness testimony, appeared to place her at the crime scene at the time of the murder. It didn't help that Vertice Brown had reported that she had been disheveled and had stains on her shirt. Even though Andy would testify about the ketchup incident, there were no witnesses that remembered her being at Pete's Patio Bar and Grill, which would make the ketchup sound like the excuse of a killer grasping at straws.

Added to that, Andy had studied Jennifer's books as part of the investigation, so naturally the details of the dismemberment would have been fresh in her mind. Although the New England murders remained cold cases, the district attorney firmly believed that Andrea Cole had killed Samantha Jensen and that he could convince the jury of that too. As for why she would do so, he intended in his opening statement to suggest that she had become obsessed with Jennifer and jealous over the only serious relationship in Jennifer's recent history. That should seal the deal. It would also add luster to his record for convictions, which was why he was persisting in charging her with first-degree murder. Two court-approved psychiatrists were prepared to testify that post-traumatic stress disorder induced by the death of her partner might have caused her to lapse into a disassociated state, but he didn't seem worried about that. Florida had been notoriously inhospitable to claims of diminished capacity in recent years.

Reilly knew that could mean capital punishment. He shuddered at the thought. Even if she just got a life sentence, the lot of law enforcement officers who ended up in prison was often little better than a death sentence. He stared across the table at Andy. His partner had been utterly transformed since the last time he had seen her. She was a shell of her former self—her eyes vacant, her face ashen and gaunt. She looked as though she hadn't slept or eaten in days. She had said nothing during the twenty minutes that he had spent recounting the evidence in one final attempt to jog her memory. "Cole? Talk to me."

She raised her head so that her eyes were level with his. "I'm pleading guilty," she said matter-of-factly, her expression blank. "I *am* guilty."

He stared at her in disbelief.

"I covered it up."

"What the hell are you talking about?"

"I sent an innocent kid to prison...Put the fucking gun in his hand and squeezed off a few shots to make sure that there was gunshot residue for ballistics. Ruined his life."

"What?" Patrick thought that she might very well have lost her mind.

"I was drunk. I shouldn't have gone on the call."

"What call?"

"Aren't you listening to me?" she screamed. The fervor in her voice frightened him.

"It's justice!" she shouted. "Justice! Justice!" She continued to shout the word at the top of her lungs—her voice like a battle cry echoing off the cold tiled walls and in his head as he trudged back to the parking lot. He could still hear it as he slid behind the wheel of his car. He could only hope that her lawyer was smart enough to strike a deal that reduced the charges against her and that the PTSD diagnosis would sway the judge when he sentenced her. If that happened, she might have a shot at surviving until he could find the evidence needed to spring her.

# CHAPTER TWENTY-TWO

Anna was pushing Cayden in the race car shopping cart, while Lexy looked for items on the shelf. "You have pecans on here; does that mean you want a pecan pie?" she asked.

"Don't you? I thought it was a Thanksgiving tradition."

Cayden looked up at Anna. "I want pie!" he said excitedly.

"I don't think you'll like pecan pie, buddy. How about an apple pie for Cayden?" she asked.

"We've got to go back and get nutmeg then."

"Where we met," Anna said.

"What?"

"Condiments—where our carts collided. Remember?"

Lexy smiled warmly. "How could I forget?"

"Mommy?" Cayden was fidgeting in the cart. "Can I have a juice box?"

Anna went searching through her shoulder bag, sifting through the Matchbox cars, the stuffed Shamu and the other assorted toys. She poked the little straw through the foil hole of the fruit punch box. "Did Rand say we should bring anything besides dessert?" She handed the box to Cayden. "Be careful you don't spill, pumpkin."

"No, but we'll bring some wine too."

"It was really nice of them to invite us over." It didn't take Anna long to warm up to Rand and Ari. Since moving into Lexy's condo, she had attended two theme nights. The first was a luau party. She and Cayden had had immense amounts of fun making grass hula skirts and flower leis out of some shiny colored fabric she had found at the craft store. She had even purchased a tropical ukulele at a novelty shop in the mall. Rand and Ari had transformed their condo into a tropical paradise, with inflatable palm trees, white Christmas lights and coconut drinks. The two men were also dressed in hula skirts. A shirtless Rand, though, outdid his partner—by wearing a bra made of coconuts. The second theme night was called "Midnight at the Oasis," for which they'd actually rented a camel.

* * *

The conversation Lexy had had with her mother before they had left for the grocery store was still on her mind. She knew she and Anna would have to discuss the fact that she was coming for Christmas at some point. She looked at Anna, who was playing Rock, Paper, Scissors with her son, and couldn't help but smile.

"Rock smashes scissors!" Cayden giggled as he knocked his mother's fingers with his little fist.

"What are you two trying to decide?" Lexy crossed off the list an item that she had just deposited in the cart.

"Nuttin!" Cayden smiled conspiratorially, breaking out in a chuckle that he couldn't seem to hold back.

"You're up to something!" Lexy tickled Cayden's belly, and he laughed hysterically while intermittently yelling for her to stop. "Well, if I can't get it out of you, I can certainly get it out of your mother!" She turned on Anna, whose eyes widened.

"I've been sworn to secrecy." Anna pretended to zip her mouth shut, and Cayden laughed again.

Lexy whispered in Anna's ear, "I have ways of making you talk."

"I know you do." Anna smiled. "It's about your Christmas present surprise—Cayden's had a terrific idea." She whispered this last part so that Cayden couldn't hear.

Lexy warmed at the thought. "I'm so excited," she whispered back. Cayden had given her so many of his little school projects since the two had moved in that she had already filled up two bookshelves in the living room and one in her office. She was afraid she might need a bigger bookcase. Her favorite gift by far was the crayon drawing of two women, one red and one hot pink, with a little green boy and yellow dog between them standing in front of either a car or a house, she wasn't sure. She secretly hoped, although she wouldn't tell either Anna or Cayden, that she was the red woman, since the hot pink one had an unusually large ear and right foot. He had framed the picture in orange construction paper. It now hung in an actual frame on her office wall. She loved looking at it. In fact, anytime she was tired, frustrated or plagued by a headache, all she needed to do was look at that picture, and it would make her smile every time.

"We might be having a guest on Christmas."

Anna's brow furrowed. "I thought we were just going to snuggle up and watch Christmas shows. Just the three of us and a big tree." They already had plans to go tree shopping. Lexy was dreading the pine needle mess, and she worried that Ginger would drink the water out of the tree stand, given that she wasn't averse to drinking from the toilet bowl, but Anna had her heart set on a live tree.

"And cookies!" Cayden had made Lexy and his mother promise to get new cookie cutters. He wanted reindeer, Santa and especially gingerbread men, since he'd seen the *Shrek* movies.

Lexy liked the sound of the intimate family Christmas Anna had described, and she honestly felt a little disappointed about having invited her mother. She could tell, though, that her mother was fishing for an invitation by the number of times she'd asked about their plans. Lexy didn't want her mom to spend the holiday by herself missing Carl. "My mother wants to meet you and Cayden."

"And I want to meet her too, but..." Anna's voice drifted off. "No, you know what, it'll be great. And my fabulous baking assistant and I will make a cake for our company!"

Cayden clapped his hands excitedly. "With chocolate icing?"

"Absolutely!" Anna said in response. "What other icing is there?"

* * *

Rand and Ari met the two women and Cayden at the door, and hugged and kissed all of them. Cayden made a face when Ari pinched his cheek. Rand took the wine and pies into the kitchen while the women sat down with Ari in the living room. "Pachelbel's Canon" was playing in the background, and Anna could smell the tantalizing aroma of turkey, stuffing and sweet potatoes cooking in the oven. Lexy sat next to her and placed one hand on her thigh. Anna liked the fact that Lexy was always touching her. And she knew if Lexy moved that hand just a little, she would be instantly turned on.

They had brought toys to occupy Cayden, although right now he seemed content to sit rather maturely on the couch and pet Princess, who was dressed in an autumn sweater decorated with little pumpkins. Princess had instantly taken a liking to him. In fact, she was licking Cayden so much that Anna feared she might like his taste and take a bite.

"So, how are things with the lovebirds?" Rand asked, placing a glass of white wine in front of each of the women. A beautiful tray of appetizers rested on the marble coffee table, along with a small glass bowl of cashews. Lexy made a plate of smoked Gouda on wheat crackers.

Anna smiled at her partner, who seemed to have a bottomless stomach. She was always hungry—probably because she constantly denied herself what she really wanted. Anna thought of the night before, when she and Cayden had made ice cream sundaes, piled high with hot fudge, sprinkles and whipped topping. She had tried to get Lexy involved, but she only whined about how it would go right to her thighs. There they were, eating away, with Lexy looking on like a beaten puppy. Anna couldn't help but feed her. She scooped some of the ice cream and fudge onto her spoon and forced it between Lexy's stubborn lips. In the process, she had smeared much of it on her chin, around her mouth and on the tip of her nose. "As in love as ever," she answered Rand as she lingered on the memory of Lexy's ice cream-dotted chin.

Cayden, apparently seeing Lexy make her plate, became interested in the appetizers. His body slid off the couch as though it was a waterslide and he made his way over to the coffee table. Mimicking Lexy, he put a wheat cracker on his plate. "Let me help you with that, buddy." Anna watched Lexy give him a piece of cheddar cheese, replacing the wheat cracker with a couple of plain sesame ones. He was a pretty picky eater, and, like her, Lexy probably guessed that he'd gag when he tasted the whole wheat. Anna could imagine him opening his mouth to show off the chewed brown mess that he was refusing to swallow, and say "Yuck!" Some of it might even tumble out of his mouth in horrid clumps. That had happened before; in fact, that had happened two times already—once when Anna had made him try her fried eggplant and the other time with cantaloupe.

Rand smiled. "Lexy, you amaze me. A year ago, I would have never predicted that you and your partner and her *child* would be spending Thanksgiving here with us."

"Speaking of…" Anna said, taking Lexy's hand in hers.

Everyone's attention fell on her. She swallowed hard and tried to steady her trembling fingers as she reached for the little velvet pouch in the pocket of her blazer. With her heart racing, she kneeled down in front of her lover.

"Lexy Strayer," she said. She tried to remember the words she'd rehearsed with Cayden that morning, the words she'd written, crossed out, and rewritten multiple times since picking up the ring at the jeweler's weeks before. But they didn't come. She had no words. No words but one. *Love.* Tears welled in her eyes. Her throat swelled. "Marry me?" she managed. She bit her lip, thinking that her planned speech had been much more romantic than that.

Before she knew what was happening, Lexy was holding her in her arms. "Yes," Lexy said. "Yes, I would love to marry you!" Rand and Ari sighed in unison.

"You didn't even look at the ring," Anna whispered.

"Oh, right." Lexy laughed. Anna watched her eyes grow wide as she pulled the little pouch open. "Oh, Anna, it's beautiful!" she said, slipping it on her finger and turning her hand to admire it in the light.

"I love you." Anna smiled. "So much."

"I love you too." Lexy pulled her into an embrace and they kissed.

"Cooties!" Cayden shouted, causing the women to separate.

"Cooties?" They both looked at each other with raised eyebrows.

"Tommy at school says kissing girls gives you Cooties."

Rand laughed. "I completely agree, kiddo!"

Lexy and Anna smiled, thinking of all that they had to be thankful for.

# CHAPTER TWENTY-THREE

High-pitched laughter sounded from the hallway.

"Is he up already?" Lexy's mother, Betty, asked.

"He was probably listening for the sound of reindeer hooves on the rooftop all night. I doubt he slept," Anna said as she poured their coffee. Although it had taken her less than a month to master the French press, she'd still purchased a regular coffeemaker, and it was that she was using this morning. The flavor of the coffee was German Chocolate Cake. Cayden had picked it out, solely on the basis of the word *cake* in the title.

"I'm so glad that Lexy's met you," Betty said, patting Anna's hand. "I've never seen her so happy."

Anna smiled. "Don't let her fool you. I'm the lucky one," she said.

"After Lexy lost Jules, I was afraid she'd never come back. It was like she had died along with her."

It was rare that Anna ever heard anything about Jules. Anytime she broached the subject, Lexy seemed resistant. "She doesn't talk about it much."

"No, I know. She's stubborn, that one. Always has been. Why, I remember her standing with her hands on her hips, a scowl on her face. She must have been only five or six at the time. And there she was, mad as hell and demanding to know the truth about the Tooth Fairy. Can you imagine? I didn't know what to do. If I told her, I could ruin the magical innocence of childish imagination. If I didn't and she found out, I could destroy her trust in me."

"What did you do?"

"I ignored her, of course." She laughed. "Like any good parent would. I just continued to stir the macaroni and cheese. Lexy stomped her feet melodramatically. And all I said was 'You better go get ready for dinner.' She was absolutely fuming with anger, but the next day, there was her tooth under the pillow. We're funny creatures, we humans. We say that we want the truth; in fact, we demand it, but when it comes down to it, we're probably better off just believing what we need to." A smile broke out on Betty's face as her eyes looked off at nothing in particular.

Whenever Betty smiled, Anna saw the resemblance. She could also see where Lexy got her pretty brown eyes and long lashes. Fortunately, fashion sense—or lack thereof—didn't seem to be a genetic trait as well. Because Betty was wearing a pantsuit with a hideous dark green, yellow and brown floral print that reminded Anna of seventies wallpaper.

"You two have such a beautiful family." Betty said this with so much heartfelt emotion that Anna couldn't help but enclose her in a hug.

Without warning, the cyclone that was her son zipped through the French doors and landed in her lap, causing her to almost spill her coffee.

"Someone's a little excited!" Anna looked up to find Lexy leaning against the doorframe smiling. Her heart swelled at the sight.

"That's the understatement of the year," she said, kissing her son.

The three women and Cayden retired to the living room. Cayden's eyes grew wide with surprise when he saw all the wrapped presents under the tree. Anna watched him turn to study the half-eaten cookie and empty milk glass that he had left for Santa Claus the night before. His face broke out in a smile. "It looks like Santa did make it even though we don't have a chimney," she said. He had brought up the chimney dilemma a week before Christmas, while they were watching *Rudolph* on television. Thinking fast, Anna had said that Santa used windows in Florida and that they were supposed to leave one unlocked for him. She had to pry Cayden's cheek from the window glass that evening.

Anna was surprised when the first present Cayden picked up was the one for Lexy. He had wrapped it himself and it showed. It had far too much tape and too little paper.

"My goodness," Lexy said, admiring the gift Cayden placed in her lap. "Who wrapped this gorgeous present?" Cayden's hand shot up in the air. "Well, this is just the most beautiful thing I've ever seen!" Cayden smiled proudly.

When Lexy finished getting most of the wrapping off, she turned the frame around in her fingers and then looked to Anna. "I don't understand."

"It's a legal filing with the court requesting that you be granted joint guardianship of Cayden." Anna smiled. "It was Cayden's idea."

Anna watched Lexy's now watery eyes fall on her son. He was jumping up and down excitedly.

"I wanted you to become my second mommy!" he said.

Lexy wrapped her arms around him. "This is the best present I know I'll ever get," she said, kissing his cheek.

Cayden threw wrapping paper everywhere as he tore into his presents. The living room looked like it had experienced a volcanic eruption of bows and paper. Anna remembered having imagined this very Rockwellian scene before she was sure that Lexy loved her. She grabbed hold of her wife's hand, laced their fingers together, and watched their son, Cayden, experience the joy of Christmas.

* * *

Anna could barely keep her body still. Her back was hurting, and she could feel a cramp starting in her shoulder. "How much longer?" she asked.

"Just a few more minutes. I just want to get your hand right." Lexy used a wire tool to shave some extra clay off the figure's knuckle. As she looked on at Anna's delicate fingers and saw the glint of the gold wedding band, she smiled to herself.

"Seriously, Lex, I'm gonna need a chiropractor after this! And I have to pee!"

"Think of Michelangelo and the sacrifices he made for art's sake!" Lexy laughed. "Besides, you volunteered to pose."

"Yeah, but I thought it would be, like, an hour, not a whole day affair!"

Lexy laughed again and threw a tiny ball of clay at Anna. It bounced off her cheek.

Anna laughed too, but her expression quickly grew mischievous. "Oh yeah?" Anna finally let her arm fall back into a normal position and sighed with relief. "Two can play at that game, Professor Strayer." She pounced like a cat, but Lexy moved in the nick of time, spilling the water bowl that had been resting on the little table she used for her supplies.

"Now look what you've done! You're going to have to clean that up!" She laughed and threw another piece of clay at Anna. She was hit this time in the stomach.

"Oh, you are going to get it!" Anna growled, holding her hands out like animal claws.

"Come and get me then!" Lexy sprinted toward the door.

Anna caught up with her in the hallway, knocking her body down. She climbed on top of her, pinning her thrashing arms and legs with her hands and knees. "Either you submit, or I ravish you!"

"Boy, that's a tough one!" Lexy smiled. "I refuse to submit!"

Anna's playful expression grew serious as she stared into Lexy's deep brown eyes. "I love you so much," she said and then leaned in and kissed her wife.

# CHAPTER TWENTY-FOUR

Thanks to masterful maneuvering on her lawyer's part when Andy pled guilty, as she insisted on doing, it was to second-degree murder. That avoided a trial, but the sentencing hearing created a media sensation on its own. The star witness for the defense, Dr. Lenar, testified that Andy was in a disassociated state at the time of the murder and "could not have fully appreciated the nature of the act or its consequences," an opinion backed by the finding of two court-appointed psychiatrists that Andy was suffering from PTSD.

That might have ended the matter, but the DA insisted on requiring Andy to testify. When she took the stand, she started rambling about Seth and the shooting. At one point, she quoted lines from *Macbeth*. That, together with her agitated movements, caused the judge to warn her that she would be held in contempt if she didn't limit her responses to the questions asked. Despite the reprimand, she continued her incoherent confession and had to be forcibly removed from the courtroom.

Given the alternatives, Andy was lucky to be sentenced to only fifteen years. *Lucky*, however, is not how she would have described it. She wished that they had just killed her rather than lock her up in this place. The cold cement, the iron bars, the sounds at night like strangled animals, the overwhelming guilt in her heart and that coppery blood smell that followed her wherever she went—it was more than she thought she could bear.

Patrick came to visit her at least once a month. On one particular visit, she was surprised by his expression—the corners of his lips were curled into a cat-ate-the-canary smile. He was practically bouncing in his seat as she got settled behind the glass wall and picked up the phone.

"Jensen's boyfriend found a photo!" he blurted. "The missing snow globe—it was a souvenir, from Aspen, Colorado!"

"Hello, Patrick," she said.

"All we have to do now is find out when Samantha was there and with whom. The globe had to mean something to the killer. Or else why would he or she take it?"

"How's the wife and kids?"

"Don't you get it, Andy? This could lead to a retrial and your exoneration!"

She shrugged. "I honestly don't care."

She wished he'd just give up and let her rot—pay her debt. She would have asked to go back to her cell, but there was still five minutes left of visiting time and she didn't want to waste it. She stared, unhearing, out the window at the sun for the remainder of Patrick's visit.

Patrick had a final message for her before he left, something he read from a notebook he pulled from his back pocket. "'Screw your courage to the sticking place,'" he said, "'and we'll not fail.'"

Andy hid her discomfort. He had obviously chosen the quotation to inspire her to think positively about the future—about the prospect of finding the real killer, thereby proving her innocence.

It was sweet of him, but what he hadn't realized was that Lady Macbeth had spoken those words in an attempt to solidify her husband's resolve to kill an innocent man and to frame the king's servants for the murder. The quote didn't make Andy feel positive about the future. Neither did the news about Aspen and the snow globe. Instead, they reminded her of what she'd done: killed an innocent man and framed a boy for his death.

It was about a year into her sentence when she received the package in the mail. She rarely got mail from anyone, and this package had no return address. She didn't need to remove any packing tape; all mail was searched by the guards for drugs, razor blades and anything that could otherwise be fashioned into some sort of weapon. She just unfolded the already open cardboard flaps of the box. There was a paperback book inside. On the front cover was the slightly raised image of a silver police badge. It had been cut almost completely in two, and blood was pouring from the resulting gaping wound. The title, written in red dripping letters, was *Diamond Lure*. The author's bio and picture were on the back cover. Jennifer's hair was slightly shorter. Andy stared at the blue eyes, which looked nothing like the ocean and very much like ice. She felt coldness creep into her bones and she shivered.

\* \* \*

Jennifer was sitting in the Audi dealership, waiting for the car salesman to return with the paperwork. He had expected to have to haggle with her over the price of the sunroof, but she didn't play along. She didn't care how much it cost. You didn't have to when you had your very own wish-granting Star. She would cover whatever price he quoted her—or else.

She smiled wryly and shook her head. When she met Star Brandenberg at a writer's retreat five years ago, she'd only been intent on getting her into bed. In the process of pumping her full of margaritas in the hotel bar, though, she'd hit the mother lode.

Star's eyes had been glossy and unfocused as she reached her tongue out to taste the salt rim of her glass. "You have any secrets, Jenny?"

"It's Jennifer." She had smiled despite having already corrected the woman three times. "And no, I'm an open book."

"Well, I have a real whopper!" She laughed and almost fell out of her seat. Jennifer caught her by the elbow.

"Oh yeah? And what's your secret, Star Bright?"

"I can't tell you, silly. It's a *secret*!" Star pressed a finger to her lips.

Jennifer leaned closer. "You can tell *me*." She smiled seductively.

"Promise you won't tell?" she slurred.

"I promise." Jennifer made a show of crossing her chest with her fingers.

Star leaned closer and whispered, "I didn't write my first book."

"*What?* What do you mean?"

"It was my college roommate's. Well, half of it, anyway." Star looked down and studied the bar. "She died—an overdose," she said. "Her parents…They were collecting her belongings, and I…well…I should have given them her laptop, but…the book was good. Really good. And they didn't even know she was working on it."

"*You* finished it?"

Star nodded.

"And you didn't give her credit?"

"I wanted to…afterward, but at that point I'd already become a success and I just…" Her voice trailed off, her expression weighed down with regret.

Since that night at the bar, Star Brandenberg had wired Jennifer money any time she'd asked. And she asked often. Cars, clothing, furniture—all financed by Star, who, despite having published three novels since, had never been able to re-create the success of the first one, written by a dead girl and nominated for a Pulitzer.

Growing impatient with waiting for him, Jennifer glanced at the partition behind which the car salesman had disappeared and then at the television in the dealership's service waiting area. Her eyes were pulled to the screen by a scrolling headline about Lady Macbeth and the image of Andy in an orange jumpsuit and handcuffs, her left eye blackened and her bottom lip cut. "Lady Macbeth." That was how the media had come to refer to Andy after her manic performance at the hearing. Jennifer wished that she had thought of the moniker herself so that she could use it in one of her books. Apparently Andy was being transferred to a different facility, "for her own safety," the newscaster said. Jennifer felt a twinge of sympathy as she remembered that day at the Blue Parrot.

She had been surprised by just how much blood there was. She had read when researching for one of her books that the human body contained six quarts of blood. It looked like there was a lot more than that though. The Oriental rug had been completely saturated, and when she stepped on it, it felt like a sponge under her feet.

Having finished with Samantha, she lowered the volume on the stereo. She hadn't had time to choose a station, and the heavy metal was giving her a headache. She meticulously cleaned up after herself, changing into some of Samantha's clean clothing and depositing her own blood-soaked outfit in a garbage bag, which she would later load into the trunk of her car and take back to the cottage with her to burn in the incinerator.

When she heard the knock at the door, she jumped. If it was the fiancé, she'd have to dispose of him too. Immediately, she chastised herself for being stupid; he wouldn't knock on his own apartment door. She went to the door, walking cautiously and as quietly as she could manage in Samantha's heels, which were half a size too large for her feet. Her heel kept slipping out of the back. She had always been extremely careful to not be seen by anyone so as not to be undone by some witness, but now, fearing that a cleaning woman or Blue Parrot employee might have a key to get in, she peered through the door's peephole.

When she saw Andy Cole standing outside Samantha Jensen's apartment, her palms broke out in a sweat and her heartbeat quickened. What was she doing here? Was she stalking her? One way or the other, she was going to have to get rid of her since Andy had probably followed her all the way to Key West and could place her here at the scene.

She retrieved a letter opener from an antique-looking mahogany desk in the foyer, and, holding it behind her back in her right hand, opened the door, preparing to strike if necessary.

Andy had been confused, however, not recognizing her, not knowing where she was or even who she was. Had she received a blow to the head or been in a car accident? Jennifer couldn't see any injuries. Then again she honestly didn't care what had brought Andy Cole to Samantha Jensen's door. What mattered to Jennifer was that she needed to get the woman as far away from the apartment as possible and neutralize her.

"Let's take a walk on the beach, and see if I can help you sort things out," she suggested and was surprised that Andy complied so readily.

She had had to think fast. Andy's memory would return at some point, she assumed. She would either have to eliminate her, which would be no easy task to do undetected, or... What if she could get something with Andy's DNA on it and place it at the crime scene for the investigators to find? Once they realized that it didn't belong to Samantha, and traced its origins, that would implicate Andy and eliminate the problem of her potentially testifying about Jennifer's presence at the Blue Parrot.

Stopping at a street vendor, she purchased two bottled waters, in the process snatching up a couple of paper napkins; she couldn't risk leaving fingerprints on the earring. After she surreptitiously removed her own earrings and slid them into her pocket, she explained to Andy that she had made it to the jeweler's to pick up Andy's diamond studs. Andy had shown surprisingly little resistance when she pulled them out of her pocket, swapping out the ones she was wearing without protest.

Later, she coaxed Andy to sit down on the sand and rest her head in her lap. It had taken only moments for the confused woman to fall asleep. As she stroked Andy's hair, Jennifer couldn't help but think that it was too bad really. She had genuinely liked Andy. She eased Andy's head to the ground, threw one of Andy's diamond studs into the ocean, and made her way back to Apartment 12A, where she ground the remaining earring into the bloody Oriental rug with the heel of Samantha's purple Bandolino shoe. It made a squishy sound.

Grabbing the garbage bag containing her clothes and gloves, she quickly made her way to the door, anxious that Andy could reappear at any moment. As she passed the display case of snow globes, though, she couldn't help herself. She took the one she bought Samantha in Aspen and left.

* * *

Jennifer's Creative Writing students diligently copied the information from the board. The heading in each of their notebooks was the same as the heading that ran across the top of the blackboard in capital letters: "HOW TO CONVICT YOUR INNOCENT CHARACTER."

"It's very important that the guilty character be the one that your reader first suspects—the most obvious one. Then you use plot twists to clear that character as a suspect and convict the innocent character of the crime in his or her stead."

She paced the tile classroom floor, the heels of her shoes making clicking sounds as she trod the same path back and forth. The sound reminded her of the metronome that her piano teacher would have her use to keep time while she played, which in turn reminded her of her parents' house and the stuffiness, the constriction of normalcy that it embodied for her. She unbuttoned the top button of her blouse, suddenly feeling as though she were suffocating, and deliberately changed the pattern of her walking so that it didn't sound so regimented to her ears.

"Dr. Gardiner?" asked an eager writer whose sentences were always too florid and ornate for Jennifer's taste.

"Yes, Patricia?"

"How do we do the final reveal then? The reader's gonna want to know who was really guilty."

"Good question. There are certainly many options. You could have them confess after they've been exonerated in a trial and can't be retried because of the Double Jeopardy Clause in the Fifth Amendment. You could have them make a dramatic revelation before dying or killing themselves. That's what Agatha Christie famously did in *The Murder of Roger Ackroyd*. Or…you could simply show the reader who the guilty character is in the end by revealing them to be in possession of a key object of some sort—something taken from the crime scene, perhaps."

As she said this, she turned the snow globe upside down in her hand, watching the tiny white flakes inside flutter to the ground only to be swept up again in another turn of her fingers. Inside the globe were two tiny pine trees and a little wooden cabin that looked remarkably like the one that she and Samantha had stayed in on their first trip skiing in the Colorado Rockies. She could almost feel the bracing sting of the snow on her face and hands.

"Getting away with murder, folks, is the best ending to any book," she said.

Bella Books, Inc.

*Women. Books. Even Better Together.*

P.O. Box 10543
Tallahassee, FL 32302

Phone: 800-729-4992
**www.bellabooks.com**